PUFFIN BOOKS

CYCLING
FOR GOLD

Owen Slot is chief sports reporter on *The Times*. He has three times been named Sports Feature Writer of the Year and three times Sports News Reporter of the Year.

CYCLING FOR GOLD

★ ★ ★ ★ ★ ★ ★ ★ ★ ★ ★ ★ ★ ★

OWEN SLOT

PUFFIN

PUFFIN BOOKS

Published by the Penguin Group
Penguin Books Ltd, 80 Strand, London WC2R ORL, England
Penguin Group (USA) Inc., 375 Hudson Street, New York, New York 10014, USA
Penguin Group (Canada), 90 Eglinton Avenue East, Suite 700, Toronto, Ontario, Canada M4P 2Y3
(a division of Pearson Penguin Canada Inc.)
Penguin Ireland, 25 St Stephen's Green, Dublin 2, Ireland (a division of Penguin Books Ltd)
Penguin Group (Australia), 250 Camberwell Road, Camberwell, Victoria 3124, Australia
(a division of Pearson Australia Group Pty Ltd)
Penguin Books India Pvt Ltd, 11 Community Centre, Panchsheel Park, New Delhi – 110 017, India
Penguin Group (NZ), 67 Apollo Drive, Rosedale, Auckland 0632, New Zealand
(a division of Pearson New Zealand Ltd)
Penguin Books (South Africa) (Pty) Ltd, Block D, Rosebank Office Park, 181 Jan Smuts Avenue, Parktown
North, Gauteng 2193, South Africa

Penguin Books Ltd, Registered Offices: 80 Strand, London WC2R ORL, England

puffinbooks.com

First published 2012
001 – 10 9 8 7 6 5 4 3 2 1

Text copyright © Owen Slot, 2012
All rights reserved

The moral right of the author has been asserted

Set in Baskerville MT Std by 13/16 pt
Typeset by Palimpsest Book Production Limited, Falkirk, Stirlingshire
Made and printed in Great Britain by Clays Ltd, St Ives plc

Except in the United States of America, this book is sold subject to the condition that it shall not, by way of
trade or otherwise, be lent, re-sold, hired out, or otherwise circulated without the publisher's prior consent in
any form of binding or cover other than that in which it is published and without a similar condition
including this condition being imposed on the subsequent purchaser

British Library Cataloguing in Publication Data
A CIP catalogue record for this book is available from the British Library

ISBN: 978-0-141-33218-5

www.greenpenguin.co.uk

MIX
Paper from
responsible sources
FSC
www.fsc.org   FSC™ C018179

Penguin Books is committed to a sustainable
future for our business, our readers and our planet.
This book is made from Forest Stewardship
Council™ certified paper.

ALWAYS LEARNING   **PEARSON**

For Alisa, Sam, Kit,
Caitlin, Hattie, Buster,
Hugo and Bruno

CONTENTS

PART ONE

★ 1 ★

THE RACE

Every morning started with a bike race and Sam thought that it was about time he won one.

Every morning at Mr Parrott's newsagent's shop – early. They started at 6.30 a.m., Sam versus Nate, ready, steady, go – and away they went for thirty-eight minutes of frantic pedalling, thirty-nine on a bad day when the weather wasn't friendly. When it was really bad, Sam would come back wet, shoes and socks soaked, and with mud spattered up his back. That wasn't a good way to start the school day.

The race record was thirty-seven minutes and twelve seconds, and it was Sam who held it. The day he set it, he flew on his bike through the roads like a maniac; that was the day when the wind and every single traffic light seemed to be in his favour. He'd thrashed Nate easily. But that was a month ago, and his winning streak had pretty much ended there. Now it seemed he was losing more than he won – and that meant that he was not only losing the race but money too.

This was what happened every day at this shop on the edge of the Peak District: two fourteen-year-olds doing two newspaper rounds raced each other on their bikes. At the newsagent's, which was called Anything & Everything, Mr Parrott would always have his customers' newspapers laid out in two piles, all in perfect order. He was very precise. On the left was the pile for what he called the 'west circuit' and on the right was the pile for the 'east circuit'. Sam and Nate would take one each.

'Which do you fancy today, Nate?' Sam asked. 'West or east?'

It was Nate's right to choose. Whoever won the previous day could decide whether he did the east or the west the following morning. The west was slightly longer, with more countryside, longer roads and fewer newspapers to deliver. The east circuit was shorter, with more newspapers for more houses that were closer together. If you did the east circuit, you delivered to sixty-eight houses; if you did the west circuit, you delivered to sixty-one. Whichever you picked, though, your time on the road was almost exactly the same. It was the perfect race.

Sam watched Nate's face. He was sweeping his hair across his forehead and staring out of the shop window, checking the weather. Upstairs, in the kitchen above their heads, Sam could hear Mr Parrott starting to make breakfast for his family; he heard the kettle whistling; he heard Mr Parrott yelling to wake up his wife and kids: 'C'mon, you Dozy Dogs!' He always called them Dozy Dogs or Lazy Lizards, or sometimes Weary Wildebeest or Cuddly Kittens. And then he'd laugh heartily. When he was with his family, Mr Parrott was a happy man. Loud and happy. Sam really liked him.

At that moment Sam knew exactly what was going through Nate's mind. If it was a good weather day, Nate would pick the west circuit; it was longer but there were less stops so you could really pick up speed and race it. However, if it was a bad weather day, Nate would avoid the west – he wouldn't want to climb Freshton Hill in the wet, not dragging that newspaper trailer behind him, and worse was the wind that blew into your face when you got to the top. But today it wasn't easy to decide as the weather was neither good nor bad.

Sam, though, knew exactly which route he wanted; he almost always wanted the west circuit. He almost always wanted the option that involved speed. Sam loved going fast.

'You not feeling confident today?' he said to Nate, teasing him gently. He wasn't often allowed to tease him, especially not at school, but when they were at Anything & Everything the rules were slightly different. 'Not sure you can beat me?'

'You wish!' Nate replied, shaking his head slowly and confidently. He leaned down and picked up the bigger pile. He was going to take the east.

Perfect! thought Sam. He picked up the other smaller bundle, which was very heavy nonetheless, and carried it out to the side passage beside the shop where the two bikes were locked up with the mini-trailers attached to them. He placed the newspapers gently in the trailer, and started fiddling with the cogs on his bike lock. The combination was 1968 – the last time Manchester City won the League, as his grandad so often reminded him; he'd never forget that. The lock sprang open. He was ready to go.

'Right,' said Nate, swinging his leg over his bike. 'You ready?'

'Sure am,' Sam replied. He pressed the button on the side of his watch so it was in stopwatch mode.

'OK. Ready, steady, see ya!' And with that Nate peeled off left down the side of the road and Sam hammered his foot down and set off in the other direction. The race was on!

Sam loved to race. It seemed weird even to him, but tearing around the countryside at this horribly early hour with a small newspaper trailer attached to his bike had become the highlight of his day.

As he started speeding away in the opposite direction from Nate, he felt his legs warming up and his pedals spinning faster. On the west circuit you had to go half a mile before your first set of deliveries: seven houses next to each other in Garrold Street, two of them taking the *Sun*, three *Daily Mails*, one

Guardian and one *Times*. After that, it was another mile, straight, no traffic lights, and you could really get the body pumping, before deliveries in Arthur Road and Eric Avenue.

The east circuit was less fun. More stop-start, more traffic lights, though Sam didn't think for a minute that Nate stopped at the lights. There was no way that Nate could be beating him if he was obeying the Highway Code.

They had been racing now for two months, pretty much ever since Sam had joined as the new boy on Mr Parrott's delivery team. Nate had been doing it for ages, always the same two routes, always £25 for a week's worth of work.

Sam needed the money. His mum didn't have any to spare; she was always apologizing, scratching around to try and help him out, but as she told him: 'Times are tough, Sam.' It seemed that she said it more and more these days. So when Sam heard that Mr Parrott needed a new delivery boy, he was round at Anything & Everything in no time.

He knew Mr Parrott well. All his life, he and his mum had lived in a flat just round the corner from Anything & Everything. One day, when he was eight, she said that he was old enough to go off on his own if he wanted and spend his pocket money on sweets there. And now that he was fourteen he was old enough for the paper round. And he didn't need to ask his mum for pocket money. Now he had his own and he liked that. And he liked being able to offer to help his mum. When she asked him to go to Anything & Everything for a pint of milk or some bread, he always offered to pay. But she'd say, 'No, you little darling, you've earned that money, you spend it on yourself.'

Except that, since Nate suggested they race for money, Sam didn't have so much to spend on himself. Three weeks ago, Nate had come up to him in the school dinner queue and put forward his proposal: 'Look, we do five days' work a week and earn twenty-five pounds each. That's a fiver a day, ten pounds together. If we're going to carry on racing every day, why don't we say a tenner for the winner, nothing to the loser? It'll make it more fun.'

Sam had gone away to think about it. It did sound fun and he knew that he'd be able to earn more money that way. He normally beat Nate after all. And, since it was Nate's suggestion, he was keen to say yes. He felt they were starting to become friends. At school they'd never really been mates. Nate was in the football team and Sam wasn't – enough said. But, with their morning paper round and the daily race, when they were around Anything & Everything Nate was much chattier. So Sam eventually reached the conclusion that if Nate wanted to race for money, then he did too.

The next Monday, though, when they arrived at Anything & Everything for the first day of the prize-money paper round, Nate turned up with a new bike.

Sam turned out of Eric Avenue and flashed a look at his watch. He was making good time this morning.

After Eric Avenue, the houses started to spread out a bit, though every time you got up any speed, you'd have to stop, fold a newspaper and drop it through another letter-box before you could get going again. This was the frustrating part of the west circuit. After that, it was head down and up into Freshton Hill. Sam loved the feeling of going up that hill. His bike was a bit old and cranky, but he looked after it, oiled it, checked the tyres every morning. Even on this old banger he thought every day that he'd beat Nate. But he was dead envious of Nate's new bike. It wasn't even Nate's; he'd borrowed it off Deano Wells, who was also in the school football team.

Nate had said, 'Yeah, my bike's broken. There's a problem with the brakes. I had to use Deano's.'

But Sam didn't entirely believe that. And he would definitely have liked a bike like Deano's himself, it was so light! It was a Rolls-Royce of bikes. He gazed at the gears and immediately thought of the help they'd give Nate on the Freshton Hill climb. Yet he was still convinced he could beat him. He knew that at school, in football and other sports, Nate was almost always one of the best and certainly better

9

than he was. But on his bike Sam felt differently; he felt powerful.

His great-grandfather used to be a good cyclist – at least that's what Grandad told him. Maybe that was why he was good on the bike. Maybe that's why he wasn't scared of Nate's flashy new bicycle.

On the first day they ever raced, Nate was amazed that Sam had beaten him; he kept on saying, 'I don't believe it! I just don't believe it!' And Sam rather liked that. Nate had also said to him, 'Look, our bike race is just for here. You better not tell the other guys at school. Deal?'

Sam agreed. 'Deal,' he said.

And so they carried on racing, and Sam won most of the time. And then they started racing for money and Nate turned up with Deano's bike and the results levelled out a bit. Actually, they didn't level out. They swung dramatically in Nate's favour.

The first week Sam did really well. He won three days out of five; that was £30 for the week's work rather than the £25 he was getting before. But the following week was different; Nate won four times. The week after was the same again: Nate won 4–1. And so in two weeks Sam had earned just £20 – and he certainly didn't want his mum to know about that. So he'd thought of saying to Nate that he didn't want to race for money any more. But every time he considered making that suggestion he was held back by two thoughts. One: he didn't want to be some kind of pathetic loser and concede defeat. Two: he remained absolutely, completely and utterly convinced – every day – that he was going to win.

Today he felt the same. As Freshton Hill approached, he raised the pressure on his pedals slightly and attacked the slope at speed. He then stood up in the pedals and soon felt a rhythm which he tried to keep going to the top. He felt good and strong.

Freshton was small, a village with five roads, though lots of Mr Parrott's regular customers lived there. But once Sam had delivered to all of those, he was able to begin the long arc home: a stretch of country road, two solitary houses with scary barking dogs, then a steady, slow downhill, three more roads side by side, another stretch, three more deliveries, some traffic lights and then right into Station Road from where you could see Anything & Everything two hundred metres away.

Sam posted the very last of the day's newspapers, leaped straight back on to his bike and then accelerated down the last stretch. He carefully checked his stopwatch again. He was looking good today, not quite record-breakingly good, but surely fast enough to win himself some decent pocket money.

And today he felt lucky because he'd worked out a brilliant way of going even faster. On two or three stretches of each circuit, Sam knew that if the wind was in your face it really slowed you down. He also worked out that if he cycled close behind a car he wouldn't feel the wind in his face so much and so could go much, much faster. He had to be really careful though; he had to ride with one hand on the brakes – if the car suddenly slowed down, he didn't fancy hurtling into the back of it. But sometimes, if he got really close to a car in front of him, it was almost as though he was being sucked along by it.

And today he found himself in a perfect position. In front of him was a white van going slowly – slowly for a car, fast for a cyclist – and, pedalling like fury, Sam managed to stay close behind it for nearly two minutes. Eventually, his legs were hurting so much from the effort that he slowed and let the van disappear into the distance, but the end of the circuit was in sight. He thundered towards the traffic lights. They were green and he needed them to stay green. He could feel the cool breeze on the sweat on his neck. He got to the traffic lights – still green – and then swung his handlebars into a right turn.

No sign of Nate. Two hundred metres to go. Still no sign of Nate. One hundred metres to go. Fifty metres to go and there he was. Nate swung round a left-hand turn from the other direction. The turn was only forty metres from Anything & Everything so Nate was closer. Nate had won.

Sam couldn't believe it. He whacked the top of his handlebars with frustration. Another day, another defeat, another day's wages disappearing into Nate's pocket.

★ 2 ★

MONEY TROUBLE

That was a rubbish start to the day, but it didn't get much better.

Nate had looked annoyingly pleased with himself at Anything & Everything. He'd said, 'Good race. Really close one today, Sam.' But it didn't sound to Sam as though he really meant it.

It was worse at lunchtime at school. Sam didn't like lunchtime much because he never knew where to sit. You took a tray and a plate and filled it with whatever disgusting concoction the cooks had come up with that day. Sam used to eat a lot of mashed potato. It seemed they couldn't ruin mashed potato.

But once he'd filled his plate he'd wander nervously into the dinner hall and look for a spot to settle down. He liked it when Adam and Chris were there because they were both Manchester City fans. They'd eat their lunch together and have great in-depth debates, which were almost always on the same subject: *Does Sven-Göran Eriksson actually have a clue what he's doing as manager?*

Sometimes Sam sat with Nate and his crowd of friends from the football team. They mostly supported Manchester United, especially Deano. Deano was the big centre forward in the school team and it seemed important to him that people should know about it. He wanted everyone in the school to know that he, big Deano, liked Manchester United and wanted to play for them when he grew up. Sam had watched him play a few times and he actually didn't think Deano was quite as good as he thought he was. But he wasn't the kind of guy you said something like that to.

At least Nate didn't support United. Almost every boy in the school was a red or a blue. Red if you were Manchester United and blue if you were City. However, Nate was neither and Sam thought that was pretty cool. Nate was a Blackburn fan; after school football matches on Saturday mornings, Nate would always go to Blackburn in the afternoons with his dad.

'We did win the League once, you know,' he'd say. The others would laugh, Deano usually the loudest. 'Honest,' Nate would reply. 'I think I was two at the time. Best year of my life!'

Today, as Sam scanned the dining hall, he could see no Chris or Adam, so he took the other option and headed over to where Nate, Deano and their gang were sitting. The minute he put his tray down, Deano piped up: 'Blooser! Blooser! I think I can smell a Blues loser. Can anyone else smell a Blues loser?'

Sam didn't like that much, especially the way Deano would say it but not look at him, only watching the others to see if they were laughing. Sam looked at Nate and he was laughing too. But the thing about Sam was that, even though he wasn't in the football team and wasn't mates with Deano, he still felt he was smarter than him.

Deano leaned over his food and looked around at his friends, as if to attract attention to himself. 'Can anyone smell the Blues loser?'

Before he could even stop to think, Sam flashed back an answer: 'Probably only someone with a nose as big as yours.'

Deano stared at Sam. He looked stunned. And the others stared at Deano. They seemed rather stunned too. People didn't usually talk to Deano like that. Even if he did have a particularly large nose. They all wondered the same thing: what was Deano going to do now?

Deano could have shouted at Sam. He could have laughed at him. Sam wondered whether he'd wait for him outside the lunch hall and pick a fight. Because that was not a fight that Deano would have any trouble winning. But Deano did none of that. He fixed Sam with a stare, chuckled and then said, in a quiet, superior voice, 'I hear Nate took another five pounds off you today, Sam. Shame you can't beat him, isn't it? Must be horrible losing your wages every day. Not that I mind. Your daily bike race is starting to make me rich too.'

'What do you mean?' said Sam.

'Well, Sam,' said Deano in that same confident voice, 'what you don't understand is how it all works. I provide the bike, Nate rides it and together we beat you. Every day. And so you provide us with our winnings. That's five pounds of easy money every day split fifty–fifty between the two of us.'

Sam could not believe it. He could not believe that Nate had told the others about their daily race and the money. They'd made a deal: don't tell their schoolmates. That was the arrangement and Nate had gone back on it. And worse, it seemed that Deano and Nate had planned it all, as though it was just some kind of joke. Yet worst of all, he hated the fact that Deano was laughing at him, here in front of everyone.

Sam looked at Deano and then at Nate, but Nate looked away. He seemed embarrassed. Sam stood up. He couldn't sit there any longer so he simply got up and walked out of the hall.

When he got home, Sam was still fuming. It was four hours after lunch, yet he was as furious as ever. He didn't know what to do. All he was certain of was that he simply had to beat Nate the next day. Losing was not an option.

There was no one at home when he got back. His mum was still at work and his grandad, who seemed to drop in for dinner almost every day now, was out too. Sam dumped his schoolbag on the kitchen table and went straight out on to the small balcony of their flat where he kept his bike and got to work on it. He'd been planning this all the way home on the bus. OK, so his bike was a bit of an old lump, but he still felt a tug of affection for it and was certain that he could help it go faster.

First, he adjusted the height of the saddle and then he very slightly adjusted its angle. Maybe that would help. Then he oiled the chain and all the moving parts. Next he reset the position that the back wheel sat in the brakes; he was sure that it had been rubbing slightly. Only when he spun the wheel and it rotated with perfect smoothness did he allow himself a smile. Who knew how much faster he might be tomorrow? Just a few seconds could make all the difference.

'What're you doing?'

The voice made him jump. It was only his mum, standing just behind him, but he'd been con-centrating so deeply on his bike that he hadn't heard her come in.

'What're you up to, love?' she said and kissed him on the back of the head as he stood there admiring his bicycle.

'Not much.' He had no desire to explain everything.

Sam's mum worked in the centre of Stockport as a secretary for an estate agent's called Chappells. But, as his mum kept on telling him, not many people were buying and selling properties these days so Chappells wasn't making very much money.

One day, when she'd got back from work, she picked up the post, opened a letter and flung herself down on the sofa with a long, heavy sigh. When Sam had asked what the problem was, she waved the letter impatiently in the air and told him, in short, frustrated sentences, that the electricity bill was larger than she'd expected and she didn't know how on earth she was going to pay it.

'Why don't we ask Dad for some money?' was Sam's reply. And that made Mum furious.

'Not a chance!' she'd snapped. 'That man! What's he ever done for us?' And Sam was silent because he knew the answer. His mum always referred to his dad as 'that man' and the truth was that 'that man' had never really done anything in Sam's life apart from move a long way away when Sam was too young to remember him.

So, eventually, Sam had piped up and said, 'Maybe you could get a different job?' and she'd rocked forward slowly in the sofa until her face was in her hands – and then said nothing. Absolutely nothing. She'd just filled the room with a frosty silence.

Sam didn't know whether she was cross or upset, and he wondered if she was crying. So rather than push the conversation any further, he went down to see Mr Parrott at Anything & Everything to ask if he could have a job as a paper boy. That was four months ago; two months later, the job came up. And now Sam was making some decent money and losing almost all of it to Nate and Deano.

That night Sam and his mum had a quiet supper together. Then Sam did his homework and just before bedtime Grandad phoned. He'd got two tickets for the Man City game at the weekend.

'Do you want to go?' his mum asked him. And Sam didn't know what to say. Of course he wanted to go; he loved going to the game with his grandad. But how could he afford it when he had only earned £20 in the last fortnight? What should he say?

'Come on, Sam,' his mum said, 'I've got Grandad on the phone inviting you to the football. You do want to go, don't you?'

The problem was that ever since he'd got his job at Anything & Everything, Sam had insisted on paying for his tickets to the football. His mum used to give Grandad the money, but Sam had persuaded her to let him pay now. But he didn't want to tell his mum that he couldn't afford it. He didn't want to tell her that he was losing his money every day to Nate. So he just said, 'Yeah, sure, love to,' and then he went to bed thinking that the next day's bike race had suddenly become more important than ever.

The next morning Sam raced so hard that he beat the record. He completed the west circuit in thirty-seven minutes and five seconds. By the end of it he was panting, exhausted and the muscles in his legs were throbbing with the pain. The trouble was that Nate beat the record by even more. He was home in thirty-six minutes and fifty-five seconds.

The day after that Sam was convinced he had Nate beaten, but yet again turned the corner back towards Anything & Everything to see Nate just forty-five metres further ahead of him down the road. Sam trundled back to the shop feeling weighed down by a heavy sense of despair. How was he ever going to beat him? But he didn't have much time to think about that. Mr Parrott was waiting for them, pacing up and down outside the shop.

'Oi! You two!' he said. His face was red and the tone of his voice was uncharacteristically irritated. 'In the shop now!'

★ 3 ★

THE BIG FIX

Sam had never seen Mr Parrott like this before. He was so angry that he looked really strange. His face was bright red and he was almost shaking. In fact, he looked like a volcano that was about to explode.

'Right, you horrible little worms,' he said. 'I know your game and I'm appalled. I can't believe it. I really can't. How could you do this? How *could* you?' He was pacing up and down, waving his arms and shaking his head. A vein on the side of his head had suddenly expanded and it seemed to stick out more as his face got redder and redder. But Sam didn't know what he was talking about.

'How long has this been going on?' Mr Parrott said. Neither Sam nor Nate said anything; Sam looked at Nate and Nate shrugged. 'C'mon, you little wretches!' Mr Parrott was almost shouting now and his gaze darted from Sam to Nate as if searching for the answer on their faces. 'C'mon! Spit it out! How long?'

Still Sam said nothing. The silence felt so awkward.

For the first time in his life, Sam thought that nice Mr Parrott was really scary.

'How long? How many of my customers have left because of you? Hey?'

Again, there was a long, awkward silence. Mr Parrott walked across the shop to the front window and back, as though locked in thought. Still no one said anything. Mr Parrott looked at them both hard, with his face right up to theirs. His eyes seemed to widen with rage. Sam felt confused and horribly uncomfortable.

'Well,' Mr Parrott said eventually, 'you might not do me the courtesy of being honest, but it doesn't really matter. You're both sacked anyway.'

Sam couldn't believe what he was hearing. 'But . . .' He was just about to ask why when Mr Parrott interrupted him. 'Yes. That's it for you two. Over. You're a disgrace to yourselves and a disgrace to your parents and a disgrace to your school. And you're not only sacked from the newspaper round, you're barred from this shop too. Go on, the pair of you. Get out! I never want to see either of you again!'

'But Mr Parrott . . .' Sam tried again, but Mr Parrott's voice was too loud. 'Did you not hear me?' he thundered. 'I said get out!'

'But why?' Sam finally got a word in edgeways. 'Why, Mr Parrott? What've we done wrong?'

Mr Parrott took a deep, impatient breath. He was so cross he looked as though he might breathe fire.

'I followed Nate today,' he said. 'So I know your little game, don't I?'

'What game?' Sam asked.

'You see, some of my customers have been complaining recently. They've been ringing me up and saying: "Why didn't I get my newspaper today, Mr Parrott?" "Where was my copy of the *Daily Express* today, Mr Parrott?" "I didn't get my *Daily Mirror* today, Mr Parrott." And that seemed pretty strange to me. So I thought I'd better find out what was going on, and today, while you guys were off on your bikes, I decided to follow in my car. Could have followed either of you, but went after Nate. Just a hundred metres behind him I was. So, Sam, I know the game.'

Sam looked at Nate. He was staring at the ground, his eyes all scrunched up, as if he didn't want to hear what Mr Parrott had to say. What could he possibly have done?

'You see, boys, it's hard round here, isn't it? It's hard trying to make a living. And I make a living by selling newspapers.'

Sam looked round the shop. It was true. Mr Parrott's shop was almost entirely newspapers and magazines. It was called Anything & Everything, but it didn't really sell anything and everything. Not at all. It sold milk and sweets and loaves of bread and tins of baked beans for those occasions when people didn't have anything for their tea, but not a lot more, not anything, not everything, mainly newspapers and magazines.

'It doesn't mean much to you, does it, boys, that people around here are buying newspapers less and less? Doesn't matter much at all. People read their news on the Internet now, don't they? And so they ring me up, about once a month or so, and say: "Hello, Mr Parrott, I'm very sorry but I want to cancel my newspaper order."'

Sam again looked at Nate. He still didn't understand quite what Mr Parrott was so cross about. And still Nate looked away. He wouldn't look Sam in the face.

Mr Parrott carried on. 'But then these last three weeks I've had a steady stream of customers ringing and cancelling. I've lost five! Not one in a month. Five in three weeks! And a couple of them complained that they hadn't been receiving their daily paper from me. And I couldn't believe it. In fact, I found it so hard to believe that today I decided to follow Nate. Didn't I, Nate? And what did you do with your newspapers?'

Nate remained silent.

'Come on. Say it. What did you do with your newspapers?' Mr Parrott was shouting again, with his face mere centimetres in front of Nate's. 'No? You don't want to admit it? Well, I saw you, Nate. I saw you stop your bike by the recycling bins in Hatter Street and I could not believe what I saw. I was flabbergasted. Off you got, grabbed a load of newspapers out of your trailer and dumped them in the bin.'

Still Nate said nothing. He kept his eyes fixed on the floor.

'Well,' said Mr Parrott, 'that's it then. If you can't even apologize, you might as well get lost. Go on, the pair of you. Out! Now! And I never want to see you again.'

'But, Mr Parrott!' Sam tried to speak, but Mr Parrott was now so busy waving his arms and furiously shaking his head, he didn't seem able to hear what Sam had to say.

'Go on, out!' he shouted. 'Clear off!'

Outside the shop, Nate unhooked his bicycle from the trailer and rode off without saying so much as a word.

'Oi! Nate!' Sam shouted. But Nate just carried on as if he hadn't heard him.

Sam watched him disappear down the street. Did he not care? Sam had to get home, grab his schoolbag and get to school, but, more importantly, he needed to speak to Nate. So he doubled back the other way, cycled hard down Station Road and round the block so that he could catch Nate just as he was approaching his home. But Nate looked up at him as if he hardly knew him.

'I can't believe you, Nate,' Sam said.

'Oh, leave it out.' Nate just carried on riding.

'You've cost me my job!'

'I said leave it out! It's just a stupid job. I don't give a damn about it!'

'You might not, but I do!' said Sam. He couldn't believe Nate's attitude.

Nate squeezed his brakes, stopped and turned to Sam. 'Look, it's just a dumb job, all right? If you want to talk about this, I'll see you at school.'

Sam turned back and cycled off towards his own home. He'd corner Nate at school, he decided. He'd ask him all the questions that were suddenly flooding his mind, like: *How could you do that? How long have you been cheating? Have you really been cheating ever since we started racing?* And: *Are you going to pay me back the money that you won off me on all those days when you didn't deliver your newspapers and just dumped them in the bin?*

But there was more to it than that. There was the weekend Man City game with Grandad. How would he ever pay for that now? But the real question was how on earth was Sam going to get his job back?

That morning Sam could hardly concentrate in class. Nate was in a different form from him, so he tried to catch him between lessons, but couldn't see him. Lunch – he'd find him at lunch. But he couldn't spot him in the dining room either. So Sam took a deep breath, did the next best thing and went in search of Deano instead.

'Hey! Deano,' he said.

'What's up, racer boy?' Deano said, rather pleased with himself. 'You lost another race today, did you?'

'No. I didn't actually. But do you know where Nate is?'

'Not made it into school today. He's sick apparently, but I don't believe him. I think he's just down the shopping centre spending all that money that he's taken off you!'

★ 4 ★

A BETTER DEAL

Sam got home before his mum again. That was a bit of a relief because he didn't have a clue what he was going to tell her. So it didn't exactly help that Grandad was sitting in the living room with the TV on. Sam loved Grandad deeply and he was almost always glad to see him. Except for now. It wasn't very helpful to see him today of all days.

'Hello, son!' Grandad said, a flicker of excitement on his ageing face. He started to haul himself up out of his chair.

'No, no, don't move, Grandad,' Sam said, rushing over and easing him back into his seat. 'You stay put.' He leaned over and Grandad gave him a kiss on the forehead the way he always did.

'You looking forward to the game on Saturday?' Grandad asked. It didn't take him long to get to the point, thought Sam.

'Cup of tea, Grandad?' he asked, thinking he'd changed the subject rather cleverly.

'No thanks, son,' Grandad replied. 'What's the

matter, don't you want to come to the game? Or are you playing football for your school instead? I don't mind coming to watch you play instead if that's the problem.'

'No, it's not that.' Sam actually managed to chuckle to himself. He loved Grandad because he'd always supported Sam, always had done, always would do. But he knew that if his grandad could have his way, the one single thing he'd do rather than watch Man City play would be to watch his grandson play football instead.

When Sam was five, Grandad had started taking him down to mini-soccer coaching at the local rec. Every Saturday morning he would knock on their door, good and early. Grandad loved those Saturdays. He'd arrive in a beautiful old car called a Caterham, his pride and joy and the only possession in the world that he really treasured. Sam didn't know how old it was, older than his mother Grandad would say. Grandad hardly ever drove the Caterham, he almost always kept it locked up in a garage, but he'd take it out every Saturday and drive Sam to football in it. It was like going round in a stretch limo but much, much better.

Then Grandad would stand and watch Sam play football from beginning to end. Even when it was raining, he was there supporting him. Sam never thought he was quite as good as the other boys, but

Grandad would always chat eagerly all the way home and tell Sam how well he was doing and how fast he was improving. And, before they got home, he'd always take Sam into Anything & Everything and buy him an ice cream or a chocolate bar.

When Sam was six and the football season came around again, Grandad was there too, every Saturday morning, just the same as before, except Sam wasn't quite so sure that he wanted to play any more. He was certain by then that quite a few of the other boys were better players than him and he didn't quite believe it after training when Grandad told him how well he was doing.

In fact, he started going mainly because he loved riding in Grandad's Caterham and because he got that ice cream or chocolate bar at the end. And, eventually, he decided it wasn't quite worth it for those either. So he told his mum and she said that he should hang in there. 'You never know,' she said, 'just keep working at it. Grandad says you're really coming along.'

So he did hang in there. Until he was eight. That was when he decided that enough was enough. And it was a brilliant decision because, when he finally told Grandad, he said, 'Oh, that's fine, son. Let's go and watch Man City next weekend instead.' So they did and Sam thought that was the most amazing thing in the world. In fact, it was such an amazing thing that he asked Grandad if they could watch Man City again the following weekend. 'Not next weekend!' Grandad said, chuckling. 'They're away at Fulham. That's pushing it a bit, son!'

But he took him the weekend after, and two weeks after that too. And that became their special thing. Almost every home game. Sam loved it that Grandad did too. Grandad loved telling Sam about the players from the seventies, and he'd go on and on about the team of 1968, the last City team that won the League. Grandad adored that team. And Sam liked hearing about it. He loved this bond that he and Grandad suddenly had together, though he also knew that, deep down, Grandad was just that tiny bit disappointed that his grandson hadn't been a better player.

Every now and then Grandad would let it slip. He'd say something like, 'How's your own game coming along?' or 'What position you playing in these days?' And sometimes, when they were at Man City and one of the City strikers missed a dead easy goal, Grandad would turn to Sam and say: 'You'd have buried that, wouldn't you, son?' And Sam would answer: 'Get out of it, Grandad!' and Grandad would kiss him on the forehead.

Sam was just bringing Grandad his cup of tea when there was a knock on the door. It was Mr Parrott. He was frowning, but looked very different from the way he had that morning. For starters, that big vein on his forehead had gone and he didn't seem like an exploding volcano any more.

'Hello, Sam,' he said quietly, 'can I come in for a minute?'

Sam looked at him warily. 'You haven't come to tell my mum, have you?'

Mr Parrott sighed. 'No, not at all. I've come to ask you if you'd come back to work for me again.'

Sam looked at Mr Parrott as if he couldn't believe him. He was so surprised that he spilled the tea in his hand. 'I'd love to, Mr Parrott,' he said. 'But don't you remember? You sacked me this morning.'

'I know, Sam, and I owe you an apology.' Mr Parrott pulled a long face and scratched his ear. 'Umm. So can I come in?'

'Of course.' Sam stepped aside to let him in. 'Do you want a cup of tea too?' he asked, still surprised.

'Yes, thanks, Sam,' Mr Parrott said, looking a little relieved. 'That'd be very nice. Look, it's very simple . . .' he said, and he explained what had happened as Sam made the tea.

Just after lunch, Nate had come back to the shop and Mr Parrott was still so cross with him that he'd thrown the first thing that he could lay his hands on which was a Cadbury's chocolate bar and he'd then chased Nate out of the shop brandishing a rolled-up copy of the *Daily Telegraph*. Mr Parrott laughed sheepishly as if trying to persuade Sam that it was actually funny.

About an hour later, he explained, Nate had come back again. 'This time I yelled at him to get out but Nate waved a letter at me that he'd written. He put the letter down on the counter and then walked out of the shop.'

The letter was short. Mr Parrott took it out of his back pocket and handed it to Sam who started reading.

Dear Mr Parrott,

I'm very sorry. Very, very sorry for what I've done and I hope that one day you'll forgive me. Please don't punish Sam. It was only me who was binning the newspapers. It was never him. Sorry.
Nate

Sam looked up at Mr Parrott and Mr Parrott smiled at him. Sam felt so relieved.

'So, Sam, I have a couple of questions for you,' Mr Parrott said. 'Will you accept my apology? I was wrong to assume that you'd been a part of this too.'

'Sure, Mr Parrott.'

'Good, so will you come back to work for me again?'

'Of course, six thirty tomorrow morning. Same as usual.'

Mr Parrott looked relieved. He was just about to go when he turned around. 'Oh, one other thing while it's on my mind. Do you know anyone else I can get in who could do the other half of the paper round?'

Sam paused for thought. 'Yes!' he said. 'I've actually got a very good idea for who could do it.'

'Oh!' Mr Parrott looked delighted. 'Who's that then?'

'Me,' said Sam.

Mr Parrott looked confused. 'But you do one half already, Sam. You can't do both.'

'Yes, I can, Mr Parrott.'

'That'll take you well over an hour. With school and everything, it's too much.'

'It's fine, absolutely fine,' Sam said pleadingly. Mr Parrott still looked unconvinced. Then Sam had an idea. 'How about this then: I'll do the whole of the newspaper run, but instead of you paying two boys £25 a week each, you pay me £40 for the whole thing. That way you save money and I make more money. That's good for both of us.'

Mr Parrott raised an eyebrow. Sam watched his face; it was clear he was thinking it over.

'Go on, Mr Parrott,' Sam said eventually. 'OK, how about this? We give it a trial run. I'll start tomorrow and carry on next week. And if it's not working, then I'll stop. Simple.'

Mr Parrott still didn't look convinced.

'Well, if I don't do it, who's going to do the other half tomorrow?' Sam asked.

'I don't know yet,' Mr Parrott replied. 'I haven't got that sorted out.'

'OK. Well, I'll do it. Just for tomorrow. See how it goes, yes?'

Finally, Mr Parrott relented. 'OK, OK! You're on.'

★ 5 ★

THE NATURAL CYCLIST

The next morning Sam pedalled round to Anything & Everything and when he got there it still wasn't even six o'clock. The streets were dark and completely quiet and it seemed that Mr Parrott was the only other person in the world who was awake. As ever, he had the newspapers ready, all neatly laid out. And when Sam loaded them up into his trailer, he suddenly realized how hard this was going to be: he had twice as many newspapers, so he'd be hauling twice the weight.

But he didn't mind. Not at all. He already had a route in his mind. And the weather was fine: clear and dry. A perfect day for cycling fast. He was actually looking forward to it.

An hour later he was back. Well, actually, it was slightly over an hour later. He checked his watch: one hour and four minutes. He felt knackered, completely and utterly exhausted, but he didn't want to let Mr Parrott see that. So he wiped the sweat off his forehead and walked back into the shop with a look on his face as if to say, *That was a doddle.*

'Good Lord, Sam,' Mr Parrott exclaimed when he saw Sam. 'I wasn't expecting to see you back so quickly.'

'No problem, Mr Parrott,' Sam said. 'No problem at all.'

In fact, Sam did such a good job of pretending that he wasn't totally knackered that the following week Mr Parrott allowed him to carry on doing the entire newspaper run on his own. So Sam earned £40 that week and he thought that was brilliant. And his legs started to get more used to the longer journey and his time started to get faster too. By the end of that week, he'd lowered his fastest time to one hour and two minutes. And he set himself a new target: could he do it all in under an hour?

Meanwhile, at school, he just tried to keep himself to himself. He didn't want to see Deano or any of that crowd, and he never sat with them at lunch, and when he saw Nate, he just didn't know what to say. Nate had sworn to him that he'd only cheated two or three times. Two or three? Sam didn't know whether or not to believe him. He'd also promised Sam that he'd give him back the money that he'd won from him unfairly. At least that's what he *said*, but Sam didn't know if he could believe that either.

So Sam decided to concentrate instead on the one-hour newspaper run record. He got his best time down to one hour and ninety seconds, then to one hour and seventy-five seconds. But little did he know that the faster he got, the more concerned Mr Parrott became. In fact, he was going so fast that Mr Parrott was beginning to think that he might have to sack Sam a second time.

On a cold Thursday morning, when Sam had been doing the whole newspaper run for nearly two weeks, Mr Parrott sat in his car, tucked round the corner in Garrold Street, waiting to carry out his plan. He'd thought it through over and over again and didn't feel very easy about it. But, even though he liked Sam a lot, he still wasn't completely sure that he could trust him. He was bugged by two thoughts.

One: the previous incident with Nate. He still wanted to trust Sam, but then he'd trusted Nate too. How was he to know for sure that Sam wasn't tipping the newspapers into the recycling bin as well? He couldn't take any chances. Two: he couldn't quite believe that Sam could do the newspaper run in such a short time. He just didn't think it was possible. It was this second thought that had made him so concerned. Surely Sam couldn't go that fast? And so he sat in the car, waiting for Sam to ride by. Just as he had with Nate a couple of weeks ago, he decided that it was time to check on Sam. He needed to see for himself that he was doing the newspaper run properly and wasn't binning the papers like Nate had.

He looked in the rear mirror of his car and could see Sam approaching on his bike. He felt a slight pang of nervousness; he really hoped that this wasn't going to turn out badly. As Sam approached, Mr Parrott sank down in his seat so that Sam wouldn't see him. And then, when Sam had cycled a little way past, Mr Parrott turned the key in the ignition. He was going to follow Sam, but would have to stay a little distance behind him. Mr Parrott chuckled to himself; he felt like one of those spies in a James Bond movie.

He watched Sam post the newspapers through the letter-boxes of the seven houses in Garrold Street, as ever two copies of the *Sun*, three *Daily Mails*, one *Guardian* and one *Times*. And then he watched him turn into Arthur Road and Eric Avenue. And sure enough, Sam posted all the correct newspapers through the correct letter-boxes.

After Eric Avenue, though, where the road stretches out and there are no deliveries for a while, Mr Parrott almost lost Sam altogether. He wanted to keep his distance, but when he turned out of the road he couldn't see Sam at all. This worried him. He put his foot down hard on the accelerator and sped quickly up the road. Ahead of him was a truck and in front of that was a Honda Civic, a rather old, battered, rusty red car that wasn't going very fast.

Mr Parrott sat behind the truck impatiently. He needed to overtake both vehicles. He could hardly believe that Sam had got this far up the road so quickly, but where on earth was he?

Mr Parrott beeped his horn. He knew he was an impatient driver, but there was no room for him to overtake both cars. Just as he was getting really cross, the truck started to pull out to overtake the Honda Civic and Mr Parrott could not believe his eyes. There was Sam, pedalling hard, right behind the Honda. He had been between the Honda and the truck all along.

'Clever little monkey!' Mr Parrott said to himself as he watched him. He looked at the speedometer on his car: Sam was riding at around twenty-four miles per hour. And, with the newspaper trailer behind him, that was impressive.

When he'd left the house that morning to follow Sam, Mr Parrott hadn't really had a plan. He didn't know how far he'd follow him, whether he'd go the whole way round or just do a short part of the circuit. But he decided now that he'd stay around a little longer. This was getting really interesting.

He dropped back a little, so that Sam was about thirty metres ahead of him, and kept an eye on the speedometer. Sam was maintaining that twenty-four miles an hour. Mr Parrott puffed his cheeks. Impressive stuff. And then he drew a little closer and saw what Sam was doing. Again, he couldn't believe what he was seeing. Sam wasn't just riding behind the grotty Honda Civic, he'd practically glued himself to the back of it. He had his head down and was tucked in close behind, about a metre back.

'Unbelievable!' Mr Parrott said to himself. He could see that by tucking in like that, Sam was completely avoiding the wind. Mr Parrott laughed out loud at how smart he was. Again, he thought about turning back and heading home. His wife would have the tea brewing and a nice breakfast waiting for him. But Mr Parrott was enjoying himself now. He'd almost forgotten the real reason he was here – to see whether Sam was going to do a proper, honest job as a paper boy. Now he was simply interested to see how long Sam could keep pedalling at twenty-four miles per hour and he knew that Sam wouldn't be able to keep it up long. Because after delivering a couple more newspapers, Sam would be going up Freshton Hill.

Mr Parrott took his foot off the accelerator. He still didn't want Sam to know that he was following him, but he also wanted to sit back and watch again, from a distance.

By now the Honda Civic had turned off and Sam was on his own. The hard part of Freshton Hill is the start and Sam hit it at speed. He lost the speed quickly, but managed to maintain the rhythm of his pedalling and then stood up in the pedals, pumping them lightly but swaying his body from side to side to use his weight to push them down. When he pedalled like this, it looked almost as if he was floating from one side of the bike to the other; rather than riding a bike, it almost looked as though he was dancing.

Mr Parrott gasped in amazement. 'He's brilliant!' he muttered to himself. 'He doesn't have a clue, but he's brilliant. Here he is doing my newspaper round, and he's one of the most natural cyclists I've ever seen in my life.' And with that Mr Parrott spun the wheel of his car, turned round and headed for home. He was content: there was no way that Sam was cheating. It was now perfectly clear that the only reason Sam managed to get his newspaper round done so quickly every day was because he was one of the best young cyclists that Mr Parrott had ever seen.

★ 6 ★

DANGEROUS DRIVING

When Mr Parrott got back to Anything & Everything, he didn't bother to go charging up to the flat above. He didn't shout upstairs to his children, 'Get up, you Lazy Lizards!' or 'Arise, you Tired Turkeys!' or whatever it was that he normally yelled at them. He didn't even go upstairs for a cup of tea with his wife. Instead, he just sat in the shop behind the till with the lights still off and looked around. He looked at the newspapers, and then at the rows of magazines, and the tins of baked beans, and the pints of milk. And, just briefly, he felt a bit sad.

He'd never really wanted to sell newspapers; he'd never really wanted to sell anything and everything at all. And now that fewer customers were buying newspapers, he wondered how long he could possibly carry on selling anything. Let alone everything.

What he'd always wanted to do was sell bicycles. He loved bikes and he loved bike shops. He didn't love baked beans or milk. He quite liked newspapers – but people were just getting their news on the

Internet instead these days. His dream had been to open a bike shop, but he'd long ago put this to one side and had settled for baked beans and magazines instead.

But today watching Sam pedal up Freshton Hill reminded him how much he loved bikes and cycling. Sam had been climbing Freshton Hill on an old banger of a bike and he'd had a trailer full of newspapers behind him. Amazing!

Mr Parrott eventually went upstairs, had a cup of tea and called the kids 'Dopey Ducklings' and 'Sleepy Slugs' for not getting out of bed for school more quickly. But all he was really doing was waiting for Sam to get back from the paper round. The minute that he heard him, he put his teacup down and ran back downstairs.

'Right! You! In here!' Mr Parrott was standing with his hands on his hips, yelling at Sam.

Sam looked confused. What had he done wrong this time? He felt a little tired too. He'd ridden quite hard out there today. But this was weird. Was Mr Parrott cross with him again? How come?

'Sit down, Sam!' Mr Parrott said in a commanding voice. However, he didn't seem quite so much like a volcano about to explode this time.

'Where shall I sit, Mr Parrott?' Sam asked.

'There, behind the till,' he replied. And then he paced up and down in front of the magazine rack.

Sam wondered if he'd gone completely mad . . .

Eventually, Mr Parrott turned to face him and started speaking. He spoke fast, as if he was excited. 'Look, Sam,' he said, 'I followed you in the car today. I just wanted to check that you were doing the job right. And I can see that you do it well. Very well indeed. But I'm afraid I have bad news for you.'

He paused and Sam looked at him. He tilted his head as if that would help him understand what Mr Parrott was talking about. Mr Parrott had started pacing up and down in front of the magazines again.

'You see, it's like this.' He paused. 'If I ever catch you again cycling a metre behind a car like you were doing on the road to Freshton this morning, I'm afraid I'm going to have to sack you.'

'Come again?' Sam said. 'I don't understand.'

'OK, Sam, were you cycling very, very close to an ugly red Honda Civic on the road to Freshton today?'

'Er, yes, I guess so. But when you go in close like that it helps you go faster.'

'I know, I know,' Mr Parrott said and he seemed agitated. 'It's a classic trick that all good cyclists do. It's called drafting. But it's what the best riders in the world do, Sam. It's not what fourteen-year-olds do when they have a trailer behind them on their morning newspaper round.'

'Why not?'

'Don't be cheeky,' Mr Parrott replied. 'OK, can

you tell me this: what would've happened if the Honda Civic had braked suddenly?'

'Well . . .' Sam paused before answering. 'I'd either have braked too. Or, if the road was clear, I'd have swerved round it.'

Mr Parrott looked at the floor, shook his head and chuckled to himself. Sam got the impression that everything was going to be OK.

'Look, Sam,' he said. 'If that Honda Civic had braked suddenly, you'd have gone into the back of it. You'd probably have broken a leg, maybe worse. Some people get themselves killed by cycling as dangerously as you were. I mean it.'

Sam said nothing. He didn't really know what to say. He guessed that maybe Mr Parrott was right.

'OK, this is the deal. Do you want to carry on doing the newspaper round?'

'Yes. Of course I do.'

'OK. Well, you have to make me two promises.' Sam looked at him, frowning. 'You have to promise never to do that drafting on the road again. If I ever catch you so close to the back of another vehicle, Sam, that's it, the end. Do you get it? Do you promise me?'

'OK,' Sam said slowly, as if he didn't really want to do what he was asked. 'I promise.'

'Good. And will you also promise me that you'll come and join the Buxton Riders on Saturday morning?'

'What?' Sam was now totally confused.

'The Buxton Riders,' Mr Parrott said. 'It's my cycle club. We meet every Saturday morning and go cycling up into the Peak District hills.'

Sam paused. 'And why would I want to do that?'

'Because you'll love it.'

'But what if I don't fancy it?'

'I'm telling you, you have to.'

Sam was now more confused than ever. 'But why?'

Mr Parrott smiled warmly at Sam. He'd finally got to the point. 'Because you're a natural. A completely naturally talented bike-rider. You're good, Sam. You might even be very good. And I think you should come and find out for yourself.'

Sam thought about it. It seemed that he didn't have a choice. 'Will I be back in time for the City game?'

'Should be.'

Sam thought about it again. 'OK then, I'll do it.'

'Good.'

And, on that note, Sam left the shop. And Mr Parrott looked round at the magazines and the baked beans and felt pleased with himself. But, all of a sudden, Sam was back again. 'What is it, Sam?'

'I was just wondering, Mr Parrott. Will you be with the Buxton Riders on Saturday morning too?'

'I will. But I won't be riding. Just organizing.'

'Oh. OK.' Sam raised his eyebrows; he was confused again. 'Why won't you be riding?'

'Because I broke my leg a while ago. Broke it quite badly. Can't ride any more.'

'How did you break it?' Sam asked.

'Drafting,' he replied. 'A metre behind a silver Toyota. Didn't see it brake quickly enough. I'm lucky really. Lucky I didn't kill myself.'

THE GREAT-GRANDFATHER'S TALE

Sitting next to Grandad in the stand at the City of Manchester Stadium, watching Manchester City – this was one of the great joys in life for Sam. This is what he enjoyed more than anything. Even if City were sometimes a bit rubbish. Even if Sven-Göran Eriksson did keep on picking the wrong team.

Except today Sam felt a bit different. He'd been out with the Buxton Riders in the morning, then had to cycle back home, change and leg it into Manchester to meet Grandad to go to the game. They sat down in their seats just in time to see City kick off against Arsenal, just in time to see Emmanuel Adebayor put Arsenal 1–0 up. Sam actually laughed to himself when Joe Hart, the City keeper, picked the ball out of the back of the net. *Here we go again,* he thought, *another nail-biting day with Grandad. Why can't City ever make it easy for us?*

But he felt different too; he felt distracted. And, for once, he felt there was something more important in his life than Manchester City.

Eventually, when half-time came round, and City were 2–1 down, he had his opportunity. 'Grandad,' he said, 'instead of getting a pie today, can we stay here in our seats?'

'Sure thing, son,' Grandad replied. 'What's up?'

'I was wondering if you could tell me about my great-grandad.'

'Sure thing, son. Anything in particular?'

'His cycling, Grandad. You said your dad was a good cyclist.'

Once Grandad got started, he couldn't stop. He told Sam the whole story from start to finish. He told him his memories of how his father would get up early every Saturday and Sunday morning, how he'd watch him prepare for the day, how he'd look after his bike with so much care and attention it might have been a Rolls-Royce, how he'd eat a massive breakfast and then make big bags of sandwiches, how he'd fill up two water bottles and clip them to his bike. And then how he'd disappear for almost the entire day.

Sometimes, Grandad said, he and his mum – Sam's great-grandmother – would go and find him. They'd take a bus up into the hills of the Peak District and stay there for hours, talking, playing games of their own, just waiting for the sight of his father climbing up the Winnats Pass towards them.

'He was a beautiful cyclist, Sam,' Grandad said. 'I don't remember much, but everyone said so at the time and I could tell myself. He looked so stylish and strong when he was hitting those pedals. When I saw him climb those hills, he was my total hero.'

Grandad told Sam how his father started going off at weekends to compete in races. And how he'd always win and would bring back strange prizes: a free leg of lamb from the local butcher, a sofa to be collected from a Manchester furniture store, a book token.

'Did I ever tell you, son, that my father was picked to race in the Olympics?'

'What? They have cycling in the Olympics?' Sam asked.

'Oh yes, they do.' And then Grandad told him how his father was invited down to London for trials, and how he beat everyone, and two weeks later received a letter telling him that he'd been selected for the Great Britain team for the Olympics in Helsinki.

'Did he win a medal, Grandad?'

Grandad took a deep breath and sighed, and then he was quiet for a bit before he eventually answered, 'No, son, he didn't. That was as good as it got for my dear old dad.' And then he explained how the Helsinki Olympics were supposed to take place in 1940, but they never happened because of the Second World War. And so his father never competed and went off to be a soldier instead.

Grandad looked sad. 'But that didn't stop him cycling.'

'What do you mean?'

Grandad told Sam how in his platoon in the war, everyone knew his father as 'the Cyclist'. And sometimes, if they needed an errand to be run, they'd give it to him. As they moved through France, they even started carrying a bicycle with them. But it came to a halt towards the end of the war when his platoon was in Holland. The radios were all out and his father and his platoon were stuck; they'd been cut off from the rest of the Allied forces and if they moved they'd be shot at by the Germans. They needed help and, because the radios were broken, they couldn't get a message out.

'Eventually,' Grandad said, almost in a whisper, 'my father offered to go. He told them that their only chance was if he took off on his bike. He told them that he was so fast that even if the Germans did see him go, their riflemen wouldn't be quick enough to hit him. And that was the last time he ever rode a bike.'

'What happened, Grandad?'

'He did mighty well, son. He had five miles to cover and he almost got there. And then, half a mile away from the rest of the British forces, he got hit. Took two bullets in the right hip. Lay in a ditch for four hours he did, until it was dark. Then he somehow got back on the bike again and made it the last half-mile.'

Sam was silent. Around them the usual noise of the football crowd was as loud as ever, but Sam and Grandad had almost stopped watching. 'Then what?' Sam asked.

'Well, reinforcements were sent and most of his platoon was saved. All because of my father. Hero, he was. Never got an Olympic medal, but he certainly got one for bravery from the king when he got home.

'But he never rode again. In fact, his hip never recovered. He came home in a wheelchair and hardly ever got out of it. That hip – it picked up infections. And those infections got worse and worse, and, two months after the end of the war, they finally killed him.'

Grandad had tears in his eyes. City were making a plucky comeback on the field, but he had hardly noticed.

Manchester City lost 3–1 that day. Adebayor scored again towards the end, but it had been a strange afternoon. Not because of the result: seeing City lose was hardly unusual. It was strange because Sam had never heard Grandad talking about his father like that.

They sat together on the bus on the way home, both quiet, both wrapped in thought. Both thinking about the same thing.

Eventually, Grandad broke the silence. 'Why did you ask about my father today, son?'

'Because I went out on my bike this morning, Grandad. I went out with some proper cyclists, a club called the Buxton Riders. And we even went up that Winnats Pass, the one you said your father used to ride up.'

'How could you get up that on your old bike?' Grandad asked.

'I couldn't!' Sam replied, chuckling. 'I had to get off and push for some of it. The other riders thought it was hilarious. They couldn't believe I'd even got as far as I did on my bike. It was the worst bike by a mile.'

Grandad thought for a minute and then asked another question. 'Do you think, son, that you might be a decent cyclist like your great-grandfather?'

'I don't know,' Sam replied. 'But I hope so. I've got to buy myself a decent bike first. And after that? I just don't know. It sounds to me like our family is missing something. I'd like to try and win that Olympic medal that your father never got.'

'You do that,' Grandad said and he kissed Sam on the forehead. 'If you do that, you'll make me the proudest man alive.'

PART TWO

★ 8 ★

THE MACHINE

TWO YEARS LATER

If Sam was ever going to have a shot at winning an Olympic medal for his family, he knew he had to get close to Mitchell Peters.

Get an Olympic medal? Sam thought to himself. *Come on! Get real! If I can't get close to Mitchell Peters, I'll not only never win a medal, I'll never even compete in an Olympic Games.*

Sam sat on his bike, one foot on the ground, waiting for the start of the race, watching the other riders. He always felt nervous before races. Lots of riders would stand around chatting and joking, but he never felt he could. Especially not today. There were seventy-two riders competing and somewhere in this group was Mitchell Peters. Mitchell was good and always had been. He was seventeen, a year older than Sam, and had been winning races since he was a kid.

Among the Buxton Riders, Mitchell was the king. Even though he was younger than them, the senior riders respected him. And they respected him mainly because he was so good. He was so hard, so tough. Every cyclist who has ever ridden hard in a race knows what it feels like when your legs run out of strength and the pain within them throbs so hard that all you want to do is stop. But the best cyclists are able to go on. The best cyclists grit their teeth and somehow ignore the pain. And Mitchell was the best at gritting his teeth, the best at ignoring the pain.

The Buxton Riders had a nickname for Mitchell; they called him 'the Machine' because he just seemed to keep on going. He never got worn down. Today Sam knew he had to try to beat the Machine.

Mr Parrott had explained it all to him carefully: today was the Buxton Riders junior road championships. The winner would receive a silver trophy and probably get his or her picture in the *Stockport Independent*. But Sam didn't really care much about the trophy or the newspaper. What he really cared about was the other prize that Mr Parrott told him about: if you win the Buxton junior championships, then the club gives you its one ticket to race in the National Junior Championships two weeks later. The Nationals were huge. More than anything else in the world, that was what Sam wanted.

He looked down at his handlebars and admired the bike that he was perched on. It seemed that it glistened. He'd been working on it last night round at Mr Parrott's house. They'd cleaned it and oiled it and checked tyre pressures and rechecked and re-oiled and buffed and polished it. This was his Giant TCR. He loved that bike. Never before had he beaten the Machine, but never before had he raced him on his new Giant.

Sam was now a cycling nut. Ever since his first day out with the Buxton Riders, he'd been hooked. He loved the long rides with the club into the Peak District hills. Most of all, he loved the feeling that he was good. Really good. He knew he'd never be good at football – he'd known that for years – but cycling was different. When he was on a bike, he sometimes felt so good he thought he could equal anyone else in the world.

First, though, he had to do a deal with Mr Parrott. He needed a proper bike, not that old heap that he did the newspaper round on. If he was going to ride with the Buxton Riders, he needed a bike that would get him up the Winnats Pass without having to get off and push.

He wanted a road bike, nothing flashy, just something to get him going. Something that cost £500. Mr Parrott had said, 'OK, I'll lend you the money.' He said that Sam could pay him back with the money from his newspaper round. And Sam agreed. Instead of Mr Parrott paying him £40 a week, he'd give him £20. That way, after twenty-five weeks of doing the paper round, Sam would have paid back the £500.

And the paper round was now doubly important

for Sam. It meant that he could earn enough money to buy a bike and go and watch City with Grandad, and City were now brilliant – OK, not exactly brilliant, but they had Mark Hughes in charge, new owners, loads of money and Adebayor was on their side now. So City were good; City were exciting.

But the other reason that Sam liked the newspaper round was because he used it to train. One hour every morning was perfect for keeping him fit and strong. Sometimes he'd cycle to school and back too, but the morning newspaper ride was better because of the trailer. It was heavy and slowed him down, which made it harder for him to go fast, which meant that his legs got stronger.

And Mr Parrott started acting like a coach. He bought a stopwatch and every day when Sam got back from the newspaper round, he'd be standing outside the shop holding it to see how fast Sam had been. He'd record the time and write it down every day in a book. And after a week Sam could see how his time was getting quicker, and after a month he did it in under one hour, and then Mr Parrott set him a new target: fifty-eight minutes. And after another couple of months Sam came in under fifty-eight minutes so Mr Parrott set him a new target: fifty-seven minutes.

Mr Parrott was great. He encouraged Sam, he told him he was good and he always, always helped with Sam's bike. Mr Parrott just loved tinkering with it. He was brilliant at mending it when it went wrong and he was brilliant at getting it ready for race days. Sam used to love sitting with Mr Parrott in his shed, surrounded by spanners and screwdrivers and all sorts of tools, while Mr Parrott worked on the bike and explained exactly how it worked.

One day, when they were in the shed together, Sam had an idea. They were trying to get the brakes to work a little better, but Sam had a far better plan.

'Mr Parrott,' he said. 'You know my newspaper round?'

'Yes, Sam.'

'Why don't we make it longer?'

'What do you mean?'

'Well, my newspaper round is my daily training ride, right?'

'Yes.' Mr Parrott put his tools down and looked up at Sam. This sounded interesting.

'The thing is I sometimes think it's a bit too easy. Not easy exactly, but I'd like to go further. It might help me get stronger if I put in a few more miles.'

'So what are you suggesting?' Mr Parrott asked.

And Sam explained. He said that it seemed daft to head back home after Freshton. On the other side of Freshton, about a mile away, there was another tiny village called Twizzlebury. Why not deliver there too? 'If I go to Twizzlebury,' Sam said, 'then I get to ride another couple of miles every morning.

That way I get stronger and you could sell a few more papers.'

'Brilliant!' said Mr Parrott.

And it was. The next day Mr Parrott drove up to Twizzlebury and knocked on a few doors, offering a newspaper delivery service. He picked up ten new customers immediately. Within a week, word had got round and he had another five. Mr Parrott was delighted. Suddenly, he was making more money so he paid Sam more too. At the beginning, they'd agreed that it would take Sam twenty-five weeks to pay for his bike, but after his pay rise Sam did it in twenty.

And the very next thing he did was start saving for another bike. An even better one.

The Buxton Riders junior road championships was a sixty-five-mile race. It started in Buxton, on Burlington Road, a long, straight, tree-lined avenue alongside the Pavilion Gardens, then headed out to the hills and looped back round again, finishing where it started in a sprint back up Burlington Road.

Sam knew the roads well. He knew most of the riders well too. And, most importantly, he had an idea how to beat the Machine. He'd have to ride a smart race and keep Mitchell in his sights almost the entire way. And he'd use his drafting skills to the utmost; at times, he'd stick so close to Mitchell and the other leading riders that it'd seem he was glued to them. And then, with about four miles to go, he'd make his move.

The road out into the Peak District was beautiful. The seventy-two riders stuck together at the start; they all knew that the serious, painful racing was a good two hours away. Some of them talked to each other and though Sam knew almost all of the riders in the group and some were his friends, he couldn't chat. He would've liked to, but he felt so tense, he couldn't say anything. He just concentrated on the race.

Throughout the group there were plenty of cyclists who he'd been out riding with in the past. The Buxton Riders juniors are split into three classes; two years previously Sam had started off in the beginners, moved up quickly into the middle class, and then moved again into the top class. So he'd ridden with nearly everyone in the junior section of the club and had noticed two things. The first and most important one was that he felt comfortable with them; he liked all the other riders. The second thing was interesting to him because it seemed to Sam that there was a big difference between himself and the others; he noticed that they didn't do as many miles as him or a one-hour paper round every day and they just didn't seem to have his stamina. And Sam liked that. On his bike he liked to be the tough one.

But there was of course one rider who was different – Mitchell the Machine. He was nine metres ahead on the road out of Buxton, bobbing up and down, up and down, on his pedals. Mitchell always looked so controlled, so confident. And he never looked as if his legs were hurting. For the first half of this race Sam had one simple, clear goal: never to let Mitchell out of his sight, to stay close. Sam knew how good Mitchell was; he knew that if he relaxed and stopped concentrating for one minute, he might suddenly find that Mitchell had disappeared into the distance and the race was over.

Sam knew exactly how good a cyclist Mitchell was because he'd recently started riding with him. After his promotion through the Buxton Riders' three junior ranks, four months ago, Sam had been invited to ride with the seniors. This was very unusual for a junior, especially a sixteen-year-old. You weren't supposed to become a senior until you were eighteen. It was a huge compliment. There was only one other junior who rode with the seniors of course: Mitchell Peters.

And so every Saturday, in Buxton, Sam started riding with them too. They were a large group of men and women of different ages and abilities, and when they went riding on Saturdays, the best of them would always quickly break off at the front. Mitchell was always in that group and so Sam decided that he should be in it too. But, boy, was it tough.

What really impressed Sam was Mitchell's

finishing ability. Every Saturday, no matter how hard or far they'd ridden, the group would stop about ten kilometres from the end of their ride and say, 'Right, now it's a race.' And this was where Mitchell stood out. He never seemed too tired; he was always so strong. Sam would try to keep up with him and sometimes he did well, but more often than not Mitchell just blew him away. Every single week Mitchell produced a great performance. He was not only very good, but he was consistent and reliable which was why they called him the Machine.

And that was why Sam could not afford to let him out of his sight today. Whatever else happened in this race, he knew that Mitchell would be the one to watch.

Thank goodness then for his new bike. Sam pedalled on, always watching Mitchell, loving the power and control of his Giant TCR.

It had taken him over a year to save up for this one. He'd carried on doing Mr Parrott's newspaper round every morning, and, having persuaded him that he should start delivering to Twizzlebury, he looked around for other ways to increase his salary. His first idea was a good one: he persuaded the local pizza restaurant to take him on as a pizza-delivery boy. Normally, this was done on a motorbike, but Sam insisted he was just as fast on a bike.

But Sam preferred working for Mr Parrott and so he kept on coming up with clever new plans. In

December he persuaded Mr Parrott to buy in a huge supply of holly and mistletoe, and after school Sam would come back, load up the trailer and go door to door selling it to their customers. For a while he even tried delivering milk from the trailer, but that was definitely too heavy.

So instead of all the pizza delivery and the milk and holly and mistletoe, he eventually decided to do something much simpler: he added in another small village to the newspaper round. The next village after Twizzlebury is Reakton and Sam easily persuaded Mr Parrott that they could pick up some new customers there. By now, Mr Parrott thought that Sam's ideas were all brilliant. And so Sam's morning newspaper round got longer, Mr Parrott sold more newspapers and he and Sam both earned a little bit more money every week.

And Mr Parrott was able to use his contacts in the Buxton Riders to purchase a Giant TCR for Sam at a very heavily reduced price. Sam's bike cost £2,370. Normally, it was much more than that. And it seemed to Sam as though this bike was completely different. He could control it better – so it was brilliant for drafting. He loved it.

'What do you think of it?' Mr Parrott had asked after his first ride.

Sam paused. He wanted to get the words right. 'It's as though it's alive,' he said.

*

The Buxton Riders junior championships came alive on the Winnats Pass. The Pass is a long, hard climb up a long, hard hill. The scenery is breathtaking; the road climbs up through a deep valley, surrounded by stunning towers of limestone. But Sam barely noticed his surroundings. He also barely noticed the Caterham parked in a lay-by near the top, nor his mini-fan club that was waiting for him nearby: his mum and Grandad were standing together clutching mugs of hot soup and shouting, 'C'mon, Sam! C'mon, Sam!' And Mr Parrott was there as well, with two of his small kids who waved to Sam as he rode past, looking up at him on his bike as if he was their hero.

But Sam only had eyes for Mitchell. He knew that Mitchell would go hard on the hill. It was an obvious tactic: in the very place where the course was at its hardest, Mitchell started going faster and faster, and within a few seconds the other riders were struggling to keep up. Suddenly, some of them were a hundred metres behind. Everyone tried to stay with him, but the pain in their legs got too much and one by one they slowed down because they couldn't keep up any longer.

As they rode towards the summit of the Pass, there were only seven riders left with Mitchell. And Sam was one of them.

By the very top, he was gasping for air, panting hard for breath. But he knew he had to be alert. Now he'd follow Mitchell even more closely. He'd stick like glue to his back wheel and try to save as much energy as he could. If he used his drafting skills, he'd give himself a chance of victory.

The seven riders were now heading back towards Buxton together. No one else was anywhere near them. They all knew now that one of their group would win the race.

Sam stayed on Mitchell's back wheel, but then moved over and rode behind another rider. However, he was so concerned that Mitchell might make a sudden sprint ahead that he moved back behind him.

'Get off my wheel!' Mitchell shouted at him angrily. 'Get off! Come and do some of the work yourself!' But Sam ignored him. Mitchell tried pulling ahead with a mini-sprint, but Sam stayed with him.

Before the race finished in Buxton, they'd have to go through a village called Flash. This was the last really tricky part of the race because Flash is on top of a hill. In fact, it's the highest village in England, but Sam was ready for it. He'd been waiting for Flash all day.

As they started on the hill up to the village, Mitchell led the way and Sam stayed glued to him. Halfway up, though, Sam was ready. Just as they started going round a slight bend, he pulled out from behind Mitchell, hammered down on the pedals and overtook him. If he was to have any chance of winning the race, it was now. He'd caught Mitchell by surprise, so he had to try and get as far away from him as fast as possible. Sam worked furiously, pumping his legs up and down. He could feel the pain in his muscles – they were throbbing, crying out for him to stop. But he couldn't. He had to carry on.

As he got to the village, he took a look round. Mitchell was over a hundred and fifty metres behind him. That was good. He had a chance. Thereafter the race was simple. Down the hill from Flash, and then another couple of miles into Buxton. Sam was now on his own at the front. Could he hang on? He knew he had to take risks. He went down the hill so fast that on one of the bends he nearly skidded off into a bush. He knew he was riding dangerously, but he wanted to win so badly.

At the bottom of the hill he looked round again. Mitchell didn't seem any closer. A couple of kilometres further though and Mitchell had definitely closed the gap. Sam was fighting the pain in his legs, pretending it wasn't there.

When they got into Buxton, there was half a mile to go and Mitchell was definitely closing on him. Sam just had to hang in there. Half a mile to go and Mitchell was about ninety metres behind. With four hundred metres to go, he was forty-five metres behind. They turned into Burlington Road towards the finish. One hundred and eighty metres to go.

Sam knew Mitchell was getting closer and he tried to sprint. 'Come on!' he said to himself. 'Just one last push!' But he had no more strength left. He tried, but he could go no faster.

He could now hear Mitchell, gasping for breath, straining on the bike. The finish line got closer and closer and the sound of Mitchell's pedals spinning grew louder and louder. Suddenly, Mitchell was alongside him. Sam looked over at him and Mitchell caught his eye and flashed a fleeting, confident smile at him, looked forward and then he was ahead. Sam could not match him.

The race was lost.

★ 9 ★

STILL ALIVE

Two days later, Sam was back at school. He tried to concentrate in class. He tried especially hard to keep listening to the teacher in his Mandarin lesson. Sam liked studying Chinese. It was completely different from most subjects, and not many other people did Mandarin because everyone thought it was so hard. Sam liked that too. He also liked the fact that he was quite good at it and so was studying it for A level. But even in his favourite class Sam could just not concentrate today.

He kept thinking about the race. He kept thinking about Mitchell, the way he'd smiled at Sam before winning. It seemed such a cocky thing to do. But it wasn't so much Mitchell's smile that bothered him, it was more the fact that he was cross with himself. Deep down, he was thinking about the Olympics. If he was going to win that Olympic medal for Grandad, for the family, what chance did he have now? He wasn't even good enough to go to the National Junior Championships.

After the lesson, Sam wandered down to the sixth-form common room, and on his way there a couple of boys from the year below asked, 'How did the race go on Saturday?'

'Quite good, thanks,' Sam replied, 'but not quite good enough.' He had his answer off pat because he'd already given it three times before. He thought it was funny how some people in the school now knew about him. They called him the Cyclist. Eighteen months ago, the *Stockport Independent* had run a story about how he'd won a local under-sixteens bike race and one of the teachers had cut it out and pinned it on the school's Achievements Board. That's how people knew about him. Sam certainly didn't go round telling everyone. He didn't think it was cool to brag. He'd seen enough of that from Deano to know it wasn't.

However, it still made him feel good that people knew about him. A couple of years ago at school he was just the kid who supported Man City and wasn't good enough for the football team. Now he was the Cyclist. But while it seemed special to some, to Deano it wasn't very cool at all. He didn't like the fact that Sam was good at cycling. And because Deano didn't like it much, his friends didn't either. But Sam didn't mind. In fact, he rather liked it.

In the common room Sam had just made himself a cup of tea when Nate walked in. They grunted at each other, a sort of unfriendly hello. Then Sam said,

'You got that money for me yet?' He liked to ask Nate for the money he owed him from their newspaper round. The incident was now two years ago, but it still seemed to make Nate really embarrassed and he just grunted again.

'Come on, Nate,' Sam said. 'You did promise you'd pay me.'

'Lay off, Sam,' Nate said, 'you know I'm good for the money.'

Sam said nothing, but, when he turned round with his cup of tea, he realized that he might have pushed it too far. Standing behind him, leaning against the wall and listening to every word, was Deano. He was smiling, but not in a friendly way.

'You hassling my mate, Sam?' Deano asked as if he was telling Sam that rather than asking him.

Sam didn't know quite what to do. He certainly didn't want to get into a fight with Deano so he just put down his cup of tea, shrugged and started walking out. But he just couldn't leave it there. He couldn't and he wouldn't. He got to the door of the common room and turned round. 'Look, Deano, Nate owes me fifty pounds. He's owed me fifty pounds for two years now. I don't think it's unreasonable to ask for it back.'

And then he did walk out.

Sam didn't go straight home after school and that was because he'd received a text from Mr Parrott.

Get yourself round to the shop as soon as you can.

So he did. He got off the bus, still wondering what Mr Parrott wanted to see him about. But he didn't have to wait long to find out. He walked into Anything & Everything and found Mr Parrott in one of his more excitable moods. He rushed over to Sam with a smile so broad he could hardly talk. 'You're in!' he said. 'You're in! You're in!'

'What do you mean?' Sam asked.

'*You're in!*'

'Slow down, Mr Parrott. What exactly am I in?'

Mr Parrott paused for breath and started again. 'I just heard from the Buxton Riders committee,' he said. 'They had a meeting last night and they've decided that, for the first time in their history, they want to send two riders to the National Junior Championships, not just one. Isn't that great?'

'Yes,' Sam replied. 'But –'

Mr Parrott's eyes widened and the vein on the side of his head was bulging again. He couldn't hold the news in any longer. 'It's you!' he shouted. 'The second rider is you. You're going to the Nationals!'

★ 10 ★

WRONG RIDER

Eleven days later, back in Mandarin class, Sam was absolutely hopeless. He tried to listen, but his mind kept on wandering. There was absolutely no way that he could concentrate. All he could think of was the Nationals the next day.

That morning Mr Parrott had let Sam off his newspaper round. He'd told him that he needed to conserve his energy for the next day, and that if he was going to have a chance of beating the best young cyclists in the country in the Nationals, then it wouldn't help him to be towing a heavy trailer of newspapers up Freshton Hill the day before. So Mr Parrott did the newspaper round in his car.

Sam thanked him, but he decided to cycle to school anyway. That was a shorter and much easier ride and he wanted to keep his legs ticking over. The following morning, he'd be up bright and early. Grandad would drive him to Grassington in Yorkshire where the race was due to start and finish. And that was all that occupied his mind.

Cycling to school that day though was Sam's biggest mistake. Because, while he was in his Mandarin class, other boys were on a study period and they'd decided that instead of studying they'd hang out in the school yard. And that was fine until they spotted an utterly amazing bike in the bike rack. It was a Giant TCR. Beautiful, gleaming and so, so tempting. And they knew whose it was. There was only one boy in the school whose bike it could possibly be.

Deano and Nate stared at it. They hadn't realized just what an amazing piece of design a bike could be. Nate crouched down to study it closely. It glistened. And the gears – they looked like something from a racing car. He looked at the bike lock and chuckled – it was still the same lock that Sam had used back when they did the newspaper run together. 'I bet I could crack that,' he said, showing off to Deano.

'Nah,' Deano scoffed. 'No chance!'

Nate sat back on his heels and thought for a minute. The numbers – they always used to be the last year that City won the League. Could Sam really still use the same combination? Nate leaned forward and started turning the cogs. He couldn't actually remember when City did last win the League. It was so long ago, well before he was born. He started with the seventies and worked backwards – 1979, no, 1978, no. And then on to 1968 – bingo! The lock sprang open.

'Nice work, Nate!' Deano said, clearly impressed. He looked at the bike admiringly. 'Right, shall we?'

'What?'

'You know what I mean. Shall we try it out?'

Nate laughed nervously. 'You're not serious?'

Deano gave a shrug and a minute later he was spinning round the yard on the Giant TCR. 'It's so light!' he shouted at Nate. 'I'm not surprised he used to kick your butt on those bike races.'

'He didn't have that bike then,' Nate said. He was looking round the yard, keeping watch in case one of the teachers caught them.

'Oh yeah, I forgot,' teased Deano. 'He used to beat you when he was riding a heap of junk, didn't he?'

Nate didn't reply. He didn't feel good about this, but he didn't know how to stop Deano.

'Come on, have a go, mate,' Deano said encouragingly. 'It's so light it's like flying on a feather.'

Nate scowled at him. 'Not interested! Come on, Deano, you've had a ride on it now, that's enough, isn't it?'

But Deano had other ideas. He made a gesture with his head that worried Nate even more because he could see what it meant. Deano was going to take the bike out of the school gates and on to the road. Nate followed him on foot, cursing him under his breath. Deano pulled out on to the road, thrust down hard on the pedals and felt the immediate acceleration.

'It's like putting your foot on the accelerator of a car!' he shouted back at Nate.

Nate wasn't interested in carrying on a conversation, but under his breath he just growled, 'You've never even driven a car, you idiot!'

Deano went up to the roundabout a couple of hundred metres away and then back again. He smiled at Nate as if to say, *What on earth could go wrong?* But, as he did, he took his eyes off the road and failed to notice the drain in front of him. Deano may never have driven a car before, but he'd certainly never ridden a bike as finely engineered as Sam's Giant. He didn't know how to ride a bike that felt as though it was alive. And he certainly didn't know what to do when it hit the drain.

The problem was the bike's tyres. They were so thin that they slid down into the gaps in the drain which meant that Deano lost control of the steering. This made him lose balance; the back of the bike then swung round hard and, with Deano's full weight behind it, it slammed into a lamp post.

Nate sprinted across the road to help him up, but Deano didn't seem injured, just furious. 'Stupid, stupid bike!' he yelled, apparently forgetting that the bike was an inanimate object. He picked himself up off the ground, brushed the dirt from his clothes and then suddenly kicked the back wheel so hard it was as if he was trying to score a goal from the halfway line.

'Deano!' Nate shouted. 'Stop it! What do you think you're doing?'

But Deano didn't calm down at all. 'It's a stupid, stupid bike!' he yelled again and scowled as Nate wheeled it back over to the bike rack and quickly locked it up again. There was still no one else around so only Nate and Deano knew what had just happened. And Deano didn't have a clue as to how much damage he'd just caused.

★ 11 ★

THE BIKE HOSPITAL

Sam was desperate to get away from school on time. He was desperate to get home, desperate to start preparing for the next day. So he didn't notice anything different about his bike as he rolled it back out of the bike rack. The minute he got on it, though, it was obvious that something had happened.

When he put his hands on the handlebars, he could feel that they weren't smooth, and he saw that the tape had been ripped. In fact, when he lifted his hands, it started unravelling. The handlebars were deeply scuffed and there were small particles of tarmac embedded in the tape. It was as if someone had picked up the bike, turned it upside down and dragged it along the road. The next thing he noticed was that his seat was slightly crooked, as if somehow it had been twisted. He was always very careful to make sure that every detail of his bike was finely tuned, so he knew perfectly well when something was wrong.

He turned left out of the school, trying to work

out in his mind what could possibly have happened. He pedalled up to the roundabout and down a dip the other side and slid his thumb up against the silver lever to change gear, but nothing happened. Sam did it again; still no gear-change. A third time – again, no response. He tugged on the brakes and jumped off the bike; holding it steady with his right hand, he crouched down to see what the problem was.

He stared at his bike in disbelief. It looked as if it had just been into battle. There were scratches all down one side, deep into the metalwork. The handlebars were ruined. The tape on the left-hand bar just hung down, almost completely detached from the bike.

He knocked the saddle back round into position. That was OK, not too tricky, though it still felt wobbly. But worse was the problem with the gears. He examined the back wheel and it was suddenly clear that he had a disaster on his hands. The gear cable had completely snapped. That meant that he was stuck in one gear. Just one. There was no point in riding tomorrow with just one gear. In fact, Sam thought he might as well give up now. There was no way he'd be going to the Nationals the next day. His beautiful bike was now more dead than alive, and he didn't have a clue how it had got so badly wounded.

He stayed there for five minutes, staring at it in

disbelief. Finally, he stood up, wearily swung his leg over the saddle and rode slowly back. *How?* and *Why?* were the two questions spinning round and round in his head. *Why me? Why now? How did this happen? And why?*

Once again, Sam didn't stop at the apartment block where he lived with his mum, but rode straight on past it to Anything & Everything. He didn't really know what he was going there for, and he certainly didn't know what he was going to say to Mr Parrott; it just seemed the right place to go. And, when he walked in the door, he still couldn't find the right words. He just sat down next to the magazine rack in the corner of the shop and cried.

Half an hour later, Mr Parrott had raised his spirits, but only just. He'd made him a cup of tea and then tried to reassure him by getting out his tool kit to assess the damage to the bike. 'It's not over yet,' he said to Sam when he was finished. 'We might just be OK.'

There were three problems with the bike, he said. The first was the handlebar taping. That wouldn't be too much of a problem. The second was the snapped gear cable – mendable but tricky. The third was the saddle. That was serious and dangerous. The saddle post, he explained, is the metal tube on which the saddle sits. It must have taken an almighty whack because it had somehow cracked. 'You were lucky,' he said to Sam, 'that it didn't completely snap while you were sitting on it on the way home. That could have caused a proper accident.'

There was one final problem, Mr Parrott explained: 'All the bike shops are shut.'

'What are we going to do?' Sam asked.

'We're going to have to be clever.'

'What does that mean?' Sam asked, but Mr Parrott didn't hear him. He was lost in thought, staring intently at the handlebars.

Eventually, he replied. 'Right,' he said. 'This is the deal. Your grandad still drives that beautiful old car, doesn't he?'

'The Caterham.'

'That's the one,' Mr Parrott said, scratching his head as if he was still buried in his thoughts. 'OK, Sam, you need to go home. Eat your supper. You've got the biggest race of your life tomorrow and you need all the energy you can get. When you're home, can you find a couple of mobile-phone leads? I'm sure you've got one or two knocking about. Oh yes, and phone your grandad, tell him there's been a bit of a problem, and ask if he can come round to the shop.'

'OK,' Sam said, confused. 'Why?'

'I'll explain later,' Mr Parrott replied. 'But tell your grandad that he has to come in the Caterham.'

*

An hour later, Sam was back at the shop and Grandad arrived, as instructed, in the car. The minute they heard the purr of the Caterham, Mr Parrott rushed outside but barely said hello to Grandad. Instead, he closely studied the steering wheel of the Caterham and stroked his chin, deep in thought again.

'Right,' he said eventually. 'Come into the shop and I'll explain.' Inside, he turned to Sam and Grandad, took a deep breath and said, 'Look, this isn't going to be easy, but I think we can do it.' And he explained how the wires from the mobile-phone lead might work as a replacement gear cable.

'Clever!' said Sam, who didn't quite believe it.

The saddle post, Mr Parrott said, could be replaced. He then produced from behind the till another metal tube. 'It's the casing for some rewiring I did around the shop a few years ago. I just found it in my shed. I think it should do the trick.'

'Great!' said Sam, whose spirits were rising. 'But what did you want Grandad for?'

'Ah yes!' Mr Parrott sucked air through his teeth as if he had something embarrassing to say. 'There's a problem with the taping on Sam's handlebars and I haven't got any replacement tape to fix it. Electrical tape won't do. The wrong sort of tape would just get hot and sticky in the middle of the race, you see.' He paused. Grandad looked confused.

'I remember a friend of mine had this problem once and he found the solution in his father's car. That was another classic old car. Not as nice as a Caterham actually. But the leather on the steering wheel is one long strip. If we could take the leather off your steering wheel, Sam would probably have the most splendid set of handlebars in the whole race.'

Sam looked at Grandad who didn't know what to say.

'Look,' Sam said, 'that's not really fair on Grandad. I don't think –'

But Grandad interrupted. 'Yes it is, son. You need to get to this race tomorrow and I don't need that leather round my steering wheel. Come on. Let's get to work.'

Sam giggled. 'So, Mr Parrott, are you telling me that we're going to mend my bike with a mobile-phone lead, a piece of electrical tubing and the steering wheel from Grandad's car? You can't be serious!'

'Funny, isn't it?' Mr Parrott replied. 'And I can't say for sure that it'll work, but we can certainly give it a try.'

Two hours later, though, Mr Parrott was still trying and Sam could tell from his grunts and groans that mending the bike wasn't as simple as it sounded. Grandad had stayed to watch his Caterham steering wheel being dismantled and the leather wrapped neatly round Sam's handlebars. That bit had worked quite well. But then he'd gone home and Sam and Mr Parrott had stayed working together. Sam enjoyed that; he liked the teamwork and he loved working on the bike, rebuilding it, caring for it, bringing it back to life.

They beavered away in Mr Parrott's shed, round the back of the shop, which was full of tools and bits and pieces of machinery. At the beginning Mr Parrott was very chatty, but as time wore on, and his concentration became completely dominated by the bike, he started whistling merrily through his teeth. Sam admired the way he worked. He seemed to know everything about how the bike was put together and how to mend it.

After they'd done the handlebars, they worked on the saddle post which wasn't easy – but they soon got that fixed too. It was the gear cable that was the problem. Mr Parrott stopped whistling and started huffing and puffing and sighing instead. It was very fiddly and Sam could tell that he was starting to lose patience.

Eventually, he put down his spanner, wiped his forehead and looked up at Sam. 'I'm sorry, my friend,' he said. 'But this isn't going to work. The mobile-phone lead's the wrong size; it's too wide, too fat.'

Sam frowned. 'What does that mean?' he asked.

'I don't know, Sam,' Mr Parrott said. He sighed heavily. 'I've run out of ideas.'

They stared at each other. 'Can't we use something else?' Sam asked.

'I don't know what else to try,' Mr Parrott said despondently. He cast his eyes round the shed. 'That's the problem. There's nothing else in here that'll work.'

Again they were silent. And then Sam suddenly piped up: 'What about Facebook? Loads of my Facebook friends are cyclists, maybe they can help.'

'How do you mean?'

'Let's put the question out over Facebook.'

Mr Parrott didn't look convinced. 'I don't really do Facebook.'

'No worries then,' Sam said. 'Maybe this bit I can be in charge of.'

So they went back inside the shop and Mr Parrott made them both another cup of tea while Sam went online. He asked a simple question to his Facebook friends:

Urgent. Can anyone help? Got a big race tomorrow. The gear cable on my Giant TCR is broken. Anyone got any suggestions as to what we can use instead? Repeat: this is urgent.

He sat back and watched the screen and then immediately sat forward again. 'Hang on a sec,' he said to himself. 'What about Twitter?' So he wrote a similar message on his Twitter page. He only had eighty-seven followers, but what was the harm in trying? Then he waited. Would anyone reply?

Less than a minute later, he got a reply on Twitter. It was from '@cyclenut'. Sam didn't know who @cyclenut was, but he was quite excited by what @cyclenut had to say. His reply was short:

Have you tried the cabling from a lawnmower?

Sam giggled. Surely a lawnmower couldn't mend his bicycle!

He replied to @cyclenut immediately.

Thanks. But what type of lawnmower?

Flymo, mate. I actually tried it myself once and it worked. Good luck.

So Sam and Mr Parrott went back out to the shed where Mr Parrott kept his lawnmower. Mr Parrott gazed at it with his hands on his hips. 'Hmm,' he said. 'Mine isn't a Flymo, it's a Black & Decker. But hey, we can only give it a go.'

Sam chuckled as his boss started taking his lawnmower to pieces. 'I just hope I can put it back together tomorrow,' Mr Parrott said. And then he started whistling through his teeth again.

The merry whistling of Mr Parrott was a good indication of how well he was doing. Initially, he whistled away loud and clear. When he'd finished dismantling the lawnmower, he held up the cable wire and whistled louder and more merrily than ever. But then, when he started trying to fit it to the bike, he got steadily quieter. Eventually, he stopped, sighed and shook his head. Then he started whistling again, as if he'd just had another idea. However, the whistling faltered a second time. And then he stopped, sighed and shook his head again.

'I'm sorry, Sam,' he said. 'It's just not going to work. I can't do it. The diameter of the cable is wrong.' He shrugged and the shed suddenly felt very quiet. 'Any ideas?'

Sam shook his head. 'I could have another go on Facebook and Twitter?' he suggested hopefully.

Mr Parrott nodded. 'OK. One last effort.'

It was now completely dark outside. They went into the shop again and Sam put out another message:

Still searching for inspiration. Anyone know how to mend or repair a Giant gear cable? Getting desperate.

He sat back and waited again, drumming his fingers nervously on the shop counter as he did so.

'What's the likelihood,' Mr Parrott said, 'of anyone

on your Twitter or Facebook thingy actually replying at nearly eleven o'clock at night?'

'Give them a chance,' Sam said and then he sat forward excitedly. 'Look, Mr Parrott. One reply on Twitter already. It's from @blackburnlad. It says: "Hold on five minutes and I should be able to help you out." Hmm, I don't understand that. And I don't know who @blackburnlad is either. Any ideas?'

'I have to say, Sam, I'm a bit too old to understand what you're talking about.'

Sam started typing on Mr Parrott's computer. 'I'm replying to @blackburnlad,' he said. 'I don't want to lose him.'

But there was no answer this time, and Sam and Mr Parrott waited in awkward silence. Both of them were thinking the same thing: *That's it, that's the end, we can't mend the bike.* But neither of them wanted to say it out loud.

'Maybe,' Sam said, 'I should go home.' But, just as Mr Parrott was about to reply, they were both startled by a knock at the shop door. And then Nate walked in.

'What are you doing here?' Mr Parrott asked. 'You're still banned from this shop.'

'I know, I know,' Nate said. 'But I was just having a look at Twitter, you see.'

'Are you @blackburnlad?' Sam asked.

'Of course I am!' Nate said. 'I'm Blackburn through and through.'

'I don't care what football team you support,' Mr Parrott said. 'I just want to know what you're doing here!'

Nate nodded. Then he went outside and came back in, rolling a bicycle. 'It's a bit old,' he said, 'but it should do the job.'

'What do you mean?' Sam asked. 'I can't ride that.'

'I know you can't ride it, mate,' Nate replied as he turned it round so they could see it properly. 'But it's an old Giant. So surely you can take the gear cabling off this bike and put it on yours. It's bound to fit, isn't it?'

Mr Parrott and Sam looked at each other with delight. It suddenly felt as if Christmas Day had arrived early. Mr Parrott bustled over to have a closer look at Nate's bike and murmured positively. 'Hmm, I really think we might finally be able to do it. I think this time, Sam, it actually might work.'

'I don't believe it!' Sam said. And then he turned to Nate, slightly confused. 'But I don't understand, Nate. Why have you done this? For me?'

Nate looked embarrassed. 'Look, you need this gear cable, right?'

'Sure.'

'Well, here you are. Take it. As favours go, I think I'm a bit in debt to you.'

'Nate,' Sam said with disbelief, 'I'm just so grateful!'

'No problem,' Nate said. 'And good luck tomorrow.' And with that he was out of the door and gone.

★ 12 ★

THE RACE

The next morning Sam was up at six thirty. He felt a little tired, but he was excited. Today was race day. The biggest race day of his life.

He had gone to bed at midnight after Mr Parrott sent him home. Mr Parrott had been merrily whistling through his teeth when he told him to go; he'd taken the gear cable off Nate's old bike and had told Sam that it was a simple job to attach it to his bike instead. He told Sam that he needed his sleep. And he told him that he'd finish up with the bike and have it ready for him the next morning. So Sam didn't actually realize that it had taken Mr Parrott another two hours before he got the bike finished and ready and in the kind of perfect condition he needed.

Nevertheless, three and a half hours later, on the startline on the edge of Grassington in Yorkshire, a hooter honked and 114 bike-riders rolled away to start the 2010 National Junior Road Race. Sam had planned out his tactics for the day, but within a few

95

minutes they changed when another cyclist pedalled up alongside him. It was Mitchell.

'Wotcha, Sam,' he said. He smiled but he looked very different from that cocky kid who'd grinned at him a couple of weeks earlier. 'Do you want to work together?'

'How do you mean?' Sam asked.

'Well, if you think I'm going to let you sit on the back of my wheel again all day today, you're mad!' he said and laughed. 'And you're too dangerous the way you ride anyway!'

'So what do you suggest then, Mr Know-It-All?' Sam asked.

'Look,' Mitchell said, 'there's two of us here. If we work together, we can do well. Let's just take turns to lead each other. I'll lead, you draft, then after a few miles, we'll swap. If we keep doing that over the next hundred miles, we'll be able to go fast and we'll stay strong for the finish.'

'I like it,' Sam said. 'But what happens at the end?'

'At the end? Well, if we stay together, I suggest we remain teammates until the last two miles.'

'And then we become enemies?'

'No, not enemies, Sam, just rivals.'

'OK, Machine, you've got a deal.'

Mitchell looked uncomfortable, but he stretched out his arm and they shook hands.

Sam found himself warming to Mitchell and the idea of being in a mini-team with him. And for the next four hours he loved the fact that their teamwork worked. He and Mitchell rode exactly as planned. After about seventy miles, they were in a leading group of twenty-three riders. After eighty miles, this was down to fourteen. After ninety, the leading group consisted of Mitchell, Sam and five others, but that was when Mitchell said, 'Come on, Sam. Let's see if we can kill off these guys too.' And they did. With two miles to go, Mitchell and Sam were so far ahead of the rest of the field, it was now a two-man race.

'Great work, Sam,' Mitchell puffed. 'But now it's you against me. From the next bend, we start racing. OK?'

Sam nodded and suddenly they were off, no longer one behind the other, but side by side. They were racing. And they stayed side by side almost all the way to the finish back in Grassington. Sam nudged ahead, then Mitchell, and then they were level again. But, with half a mile to go, Mitchell suddenly surged forward. It was as if he had a rocket engine on his bike. Sam tried to speed up, but he couldn't keep up with him.

Mitchell had beaten him again.

After the race, Mitchell and Sam had to wait around for the presentation ceremony. They were given their medals by a short, fit-looking, dark-haired man who was very complimentary to them both. He presented Mitchell with a trophy too. Everything felt big, exciting and special. Sam hadn't beaten Mitchell, but he didn't feel quite so much as if he'd lost the race now. He was made to feel proud that he'd come second.

Mitchell was so nice to him too. After they'd got their medals, he told Sam that he was the toughest junior rider he'd ever raced and Sam liked that.

'Thanks, Machine,' he said.

Mitch frowned. 'Please don't call me that, Sam.'

'Sorry, why not?' Sam asked.

'Everyone at the club calls me Machine. It's as if they expect me to produce results all the time. I hate it. What if I mess up? What if I have a bad day? Or if I crash? Does that mean the Machine is broken? I'd just much rather be Mitch.'

Sam smiled. 'OK then, Mitch it is.'

They were just about to leave when the man who had presented them with their medals approached them.

'Well done, boys,' he said. 'Outstanding race from the pair of you.'

Sam looked at Mitch to answer first, but he didn't say anything. He just stared at the man.

'Thanks,' Sam replied, 'thanks very much.'

'Do you mind if I take a look at your bike?' the man said, addressing the question directly to Sam.

'Sure,' Sam said, though he didn't really understand why.

The man studied it closely, especially the handlebars and the saddle post, and he muttered to himself. 'Where did you get this saddle post from?' he asked eventually.

'A bloke's shed,' Sam replied. 'My saddle post broke yesterday.'

'Hmm. And the handlebar tape?'

'The steering wheel of my grandad's car.'

'Very interesting.'

'And before you ask,' said Sam, 'we had to replace the gear cable at the last minute too. We tried a mobile-phone cord first and then a lawnmower cable, but we had to strip down another bike instead.'

The man was intrigued. 'Work of genius, young man,' he said. 'You must be the second Flying Scotsman!'

'Sorry, sir,' Sam replied, confused, 'but who's the Flying Scotsman?'

The man looked at Sam in a way that Sam recognized. It was the way teachers looked at you when you didn't know the answer to an easy question.

'Never mind,' he said. 'Look, I think we need to stay in touch. Have you two ever done any track cycling before?'

'Never,' Sam said. Mitch still didn't say anything; he just shook his head.

'OK, well, we'll have to get you started quick. First things first: at GB Cycling, where I work, we have an academy; it's a group of talented young riders who we try to turn into Olympic gold medallists. Would you both be interested in joining us?'

Sam giggled. Mitch finally managed to splutter, 'Yes.' And Sam then agreed too. Not exactly a hard decision, he thought.

'Good,' said the man. 'You two should fit in well.' He turned to go and then looked back again at Sam. 'And by the way, young man, the next time you need a new gear cable, try using your washing line. It once worked a treat for me.'

As he walked away, Sam turned to Mitch. 'What's wrong with you?' he asked. 'Why wouldn't you talk to him?'

'Do you know who that was?' Mitch asked.

'I haven't got a clue,' Sam replied.

'The Professor!'

Sam looked at him blankly. 'Who on earth is the Professor?'

★ 13 ★

HISTORY ON WHEELS

Two days later, Mitch and Sam decided to meet up after school for a training ride. At least it was supposed to be a training ride, but it turned out to be more like a history lesson. As Mitch explained to Sam: 'If you don't know who the Professor or the Flying Scotsman are, then you shouldn't be allowed to ride a bike.'

THE PROFESSOR

The Professor, Mitch explained, the guy they'd met in Grassington, was Chris Boardman: Olympic gold medallist, world record-holder, world champion. A bloke who'd done pretty much everything.

'That guy?' Sam asked in disbelief. 'That guy was an Olympic gold medallist?'

'He sure was,' Mitch replied. 'Why do you think I could hardly talk? That guy is so cool. He was in the Barcelona Olympics in 1992. And he turned up there with this totally cool bike that he had invented with Lotus.'

'But Lotus make sports cars.'

'Exactly.'

'So a car company helped him build a bike? No way!'

'Absolutely. And this bike – it was so cool. It was totally different to anything anyone had seen before. It had the handlebars way lower than the seat. It looked like he was cycling downhill.'

Mitch explained more. Chris Boardman was called the Professor, he said, because he was so smart, because he would work everything out, his training, his preparation, the weird bike – he calculated everything beforehand, so that bike-racing was like an equation.

'And that's how he won?' Sam asked.

'Well, kind of. It helped that he was a beast of a cyclist.'

'And we met him!' Sam said as if still recovering from shock. 'Unbelievable!'

'I know,' Mitch agreed. 'And if we're ever going to be any good at this sport, then we've at least got to try and be smart like him too.'

THE FLYING SCOTSMAN

'The Flying Scotsman,' Mitch explained, 'is one of the maddest, coolest cyclists of all time. His name is

Graeme Obree. In the 1990s he won world championships – he broke one of the world records that the Professor had already broken. Twice. And the Professor then broke it back again.'

But the best bit about the Flying Scotsman, Mitch said, were his bikes. 'He once made his bike go faster using parts of a washing machine. He once realized that he could cycle even faster still if he chopped off his bike's handlebars! That was why the Professor said that you were like the second Flying Scotsman – because Obree invented all his bikes in his home in a small town in Scotland. Just like you with your lawnmower cables.'

'Oh, I see!' Sam said. He was slowly beginning to make sense of things. 'So it was a compliment when the Professor called me that then?'

Mitch nodded. 'In cycling, it's about as nice a compliment as you can get.'

'Wow!' said Sam. 'I didn't know any of this. How come you know it all?'

'Because if we've got any chance of ever winning a medal one day in the Olympics, then we kind of have these guys to thank. Great Britain used to be rubbish at cycling, then Obree and Boardman came along and everyone else thought, *Wow, maybe we can be good at cycling after all.* They're like the big daddies of British cycling.'

Mitch and Sam carried on riding. Sam liked riding with his new friend. They climbed a hill and as they were rolling gently down the other side, Mitch said to him, 'There's one thing you haven't told me. Your bike? Why did you have to do all those last-minute repairs before the Nationals?'

'It got vandalized. I don't know who by. I probably never will. The worst thing is it happened at school.'

'At your school?' Mitch couldn't believe that. 'You should defect. That's what the Cubans would do.'

'What do you mean?'

'Oh dear,' Mitch said, shaking his head. 'You don't know anything, do you?'

In Cuba, he explained, the professional athletes don't get much money. They certainly don't get as much money as they would if they were playing in another country. So quite often, when they're playing abroad in a big competition, they disappear.

'Cuban boxers are brilliant,' Mitch said. 'But they often seem to go missing when they're in a foreign country. Basically, they want to change country. That's what defecting is. And that's why I think you should defect from your school. It doesn't sound very nice.'

Sam thought about that, but he didn't want to defect from his school. It wasn't perfect, but he wanted to stay there. Since he'd discovered cycling, school had actually got better and better.

★ 14 ★

ACADEMY LIFE

It took Sam a while to realize it, but that last race was to change his life. It was pretty special to have come second in the National Junior Championships and to have met the Professor, but joining the GB Academy was even better.

When he told his mum and Grandad about the academy, Grandad of course thought it was brilliant.

'You're on the way, son!' he said, his eyes lighting up with excitement. 'You're on the way! You're following your great-grandfather, just like you said you would!'

But his mum wasn't quite so enthusiastic. She went a bit quiet and then asked, 'What does this mean, Sam? What does it mean for school and your A levels?'

So Sam had to make a promise that his schoolwork wouldn't suffer. The deal was this: schoolwork would always come first. But, in Sam's eyes, cycling was never far behind.

Every Tuesday and Thursday after school, for the

next year, Sam and Mitch would travel into the centre of Manchester to the velodrome. Sam knew the way because it wasn't far from where Man City played. The Man City stadium had by then changed its name to the Etihad Stadium and the manager had changed again to Roberto Mancini. But, though Sam's affections hadn't changed, he found he hardly had any time to go there with Grandad any more. He became completely and utterly focused on cycling and the Olympics.

The velodrome was amazing for three reasons:

Firstly, it was just so weird. When you cycle round the velodrome, the track is a big oval with the banks going steeply up either side. At each end, where the banks are at their steepest, the angle is 42 degrees. That, said Mitch, who seemed to know everything, was almost as steep as the pyramids in Egypt. 'Imagine that!' he'd exclaimed. And Sam did imagine it. It felt weird and at first it felt scary too.

Next, the other boys and girls in the academy were all so good, so serious, so focused; they trained so hard, they raced so hard and, when they'd been training hard and their legs were hurting like mad, they hardly ever showed the pain. Sam would look at all these other riders and think: *If this is how good everyone else is, then how on earth am I ever going to get picked to be in the Olympics?*

And, finally, the coaches were amazing. They

were so smart and so dedicated. They said things like: 'If you want it enough, if you really, really want to be an Olympian and win Olympic medals, then we'll help you achieve it.' It made Sam excited and determined, to hear things like that. He'd look around at the other academy riders and think: *Who else wants it? Who wants it as much as me?*

But not all the coaches were quite like that. One day they'd been warming up on the track when one of the coaches, the wiry, bald guy with slightly too hairy ears – Travis MacDevlin, known to everyone as Mac – called Sam over.

'What do you think you're doing?' he asked him.

But Sam didn't know what he meant. 'What've I done wrong, Mac?' he asked.

'You know perfectly well,' was the reply. 'You were riding like an idiot. You were riding so close to the wheel in front of you, so dangerously, it was a miracle you didn't cause a pile-up. You're riding like an imbecile.'

Sam just didn't understand it. He always rode like that. His ability to stay so close to the bike in front – that was one of his skills. So he tried to ignore Mac – except when he was aware that Mac was watching him closely. He couldn't work out why, but he didn't like Mac at all.

Sometimes when they were at the velodrome, they'd see the Professor, though no one seemed to know exactly what he did. He was apparently involved in an exciting project that no one was allowed to talk about. So Sam loved it when he saw him watching the academy kids training. He would watch intently, as if he was analysing them. And occasionally he'd then come and talk to one or two of them. And that made them feel special. If the Professor talked to you, everyone else wanted to know why. What did he want? What had he said? But really everyone else was jealous because they knew that the Professor spoke to the riders who were doing the best. And Sam loved that – because the two riders he spoke to most were him and Mitch.

Back in school, meanwhile, Sam tried hard to concentrate on his lessons without letting his cycling stop him doing well in his exams. Everyone at the school now knew though that he was a rider at the GB Cycling Academy. He became rather famous, which he thought was quite funny. He wasn't famous like the football team. If you wanted to be cool at school, you had to be in that. But people seemed to think that being in the GB Cycling Academy was a pretty cool thing too. Sam liked that. He never worried when he went into the dining room any more. He never sat with Nate or Deano and that crowd. He had plenty of other friends.

But he didn't have time to worry about people like Deano either because Sam had no time. He had school, A levels, two nights a week at the Cycling

Academy – and often weekends there too – and he still had Mr Parrott's newspaper round.

Grandad would sometimes joke to him, 'I don't know how you fit it all in, son.' But, actually, Grandad was quite happy. He loved going to the velodrome to watch him. Whenever Sam was racing, he'd tell Grandad and he'd be there. Grandad said to him one day, 'I always hoped I'd watch you one day playing for City. But this is much better.'

After nearly a year at the academy, the Professor started coming to watch more often. People still talked about his mystery project, but to Sam and Mitch he seemed less mysterious because he'd come and talk to them every time he came. And he was always very precise with his questions. He wanted to know what they were eating, what training they were doing. He wanted to know that they were doing everything right to be an Olympic cyclist. He also asked if they were working hard for their A levels.

And then one day, after training, he took the pair of them aside. 'We've got a plan for you two,' he said, 'and I think it's a pretty smart one. You two are doing so well here I think you're ready for it.'

'What is it?' they said together.

'We want to send you to Japan. We want to send you to school.'

'But I've almost finished school,' Sam said. 'I don't want to go back again.'

The Professor laughed. 'OK, fair point,' he said. 'But this isn't normal school. This is keirin school. You two are great riders and we think you could be great keirin riders. Keirin is one of the Olympic cycling events that we think you could both excel at.'

Sam and Mitch looked at each other and shrugged. Even Mitch, who was supposed to know everything about cycling, didn't seem to know if this was good or bad. So Sam asked, 'The London Olympics are only a year away. Does this mean that we've got a chance of being in them?'

'I doubt it,' he said. 'You should both be focusing on the Olympics after that which will be in Rio de Janeiro in Brazil. But you're still miles away from that. I think you're good, very good – both of you. Are you ever going to be good enough to go to an Olympics? I haven't a clue. But you've got no chance until you've been to keirin school.'

★ 15 ★

FAREWELL SURPRISE

A month later, two days after he finished his A levels, Sam was packing for Japan. It wasn't easy because his mother needed lots of hugs. She kept on saying, 'I don't know what I'm going to do without you,' and, 'You're not old enough to leave home.' And Sam kept on telling her that he wasn't leaving home at all.

But, besides packing and hugging his mother, he was also desperately trying to watch some videos on his laptop. He wanted to watch as many clips and digital replays of keirin races as he could before he left for Japan.

The keirin was such a strange race, but a brilliant one too. There were six people in each race and a bloke on a small motorbike. The motorbike was apparently called a 'derny'. And in a keirin race, it seemed, no one ever overtook the derny. Over a few laps, the derny went faster and faster and all the bikes followed it closely, glued to each other's back wheels, drafting perfectly. And then, always at the same place, with two and a half laps to go, the derny pulled over and the riders would be involved in a frantic race to the finish.

It looked very messy and the more Sam watched on YouTube, the more crashes he saw. Keirin racing, it seemed, was very tactical, quite physical and sometimes rather dangerous. So he didn't show his mother the crashes. He didn't think that would help her state of mind.

He wondered why the Professor had decided that he and Mitch would be good keirin riders. They were both very fast, for sure. But maybe it was because of their skill as riders, the way they'd both learned to draft so well – as if they spent their entire racing lives being dragged along by a rusty Honda Civic.

Sam was watching yet another keirin crash when there was a knock at the door. He assumed it was Mr Parrott who'd said that he'd pop round to say goodbye. But there, standing on the doormat, was someone he had not expected to see. Nate.

'What on earth are you doing here?' Sam asked.

'That's not a very warm welcome,' Nate replied, in a voice that sounded as though he was trying to be friendly. 'Is your mum in?'

'Yes,' said Sam. 'She's not in great shape though. What do you want to see her for?'

'I don't want to see her at all, Sam. I want to talk to you. In private, like. Do you mind coming out here for a quick chat?' he asked.

And so Sam stepped out, shut the door behind him and shrugged. 'What's up?'

'I just wanted to wish you good luck,' Nate said. 'I know this might surprise you but I do. I want to say three things. I want to say good luck and I want to say sorry.'

'Why sorry?' Sam asked, a little confused.

Nate seemed emotional. He could hardly look Sam in the eye. He started off by handing Sam £50. 'Here,' he said, 'take it. This is the money I owe from the newspaper round. When was it? Four years ago?'

'I don't get this,' Sam said. 'You haven't come to say sorry for that, have you?'

'No,' Nate said quietly, shaking his head. And then he explained – about the bike, about that day at school just over a year ago, about how it got damaged and how he should never have allowed Deano to ride it. He said he'd always wanted to tell Sam, but Deano had told him not to. He said that he'd felt guilty – so, so guilty – and that was why, that night before the Junior Nationals, he'd brought round his bike, so Sam could take the gear cable and ride in the big race.

'I'm so sorry,' Nate said. 'But I just wanted to be honest with you at long last. I wanted to apologize and to wish you luck.'

Sam looked into Nate's eyes. He seemed embarrassed. Sam felt cross with him, angry, but not so angry that he didn't also feel a little sorry for him too. He didn't know what to say, so there was a moment's silence before he remembered something. 'I thought you wanted to say three things,' he said. 'You've said sorry and good luck. What else?'

Nate paused. He looked embarrassed again. 'I don't know how to say this,' he said, 'but I wanted to try and say that I'm kind of proud of you. I think a lot of people are. Of what you've done, Sam. Becoming this amazing cyclist. Maybe one day off to the Olympics. I suppose I just wanted to say well done.'

Sam stared at Nate. He still didn't know how to respond so Nate just turned and walked away. He was almost out of sight when Sam called after him: 'Nate!'

He turned round as if he was worried about what Sam might say. But Sam just smiled at him. He knew that the apology had been a big deal.

'Thanks!' he shouted out. Then Nate smiled back and nodded his head, and Sam knew then that he'd meant everything he'd said.

★ 16 ★

BIG IN JAPAN

Leaving for Japan, on a trip paid for by the British Cycling organization, seemed pretty cool. It made Sam and Mitch feel rather special. After travelling for a day and a half and arriving at the International Keirin School, though, it didn't feel special at all. In fact, it felt like prison.

As soon as they arrived, they were given robes that they were told they had to wear to class. Having robes was a bit weird, but what came next was worse. They were asked to hand over their mobile phones. And then they were told there was no Internet access. And then they were shown to their rooms. They were called bedrooms, but, since they were small and consisted of nothing but a single bed and a few unfriendly cockroaches, they were more like prison cells.

Sam and Mitch looked at each other. No email, no Facebook, no Twitter, no downloading, no keeping up with things back home, no cyberspace gaming, no surfing, no chatroom with their mates, no contact with the Professor, no checking the Man City score, no finding out if Roberto Mancini had been sacked. How could anyone possibly live like this? And what about the Professor? Did he know that this is what it would be like? Of course he did. He was probably laughing his head off. So Sam and Mitch went to bed that night feeling homesick and wondering if they were the victims of an extremely bad joke.

The next morning they were woken up by a loudspeaker blasting out a wake-up call in Japanese above the doors of their rooms. They presumed it was a wake-up call because they recognized the one Japanese word they knew: *konnichiwa*. Japanese for hello. So they got up, put on their robes and followed everyone else.

'Unbelievable!' Sam said to Mitch as they walked down the stairs. 'What on earth are we doing here?'

'Improving our skills as bike-riders apparently,' replied Mitch.

'Hmmm.' Sam frowned. 'I can't quite see how this is going to help in the Olympics.'

'No. I wasn't planning on wearing my Keirin School robes to the Olympics either.'

And so the first day at school began. The rule was this: if you want to ride keirin races in Japan, you have to complete Keirin School first. There were 200 Japanese boys there, the 200 best young riders in the country. And Sam and Mitch.

'Why would anyone want to come to this place?' Sam asked under his breath.

'Because they want to become millionaires,' Mitch replied.

'You what?'

'Honestly, mate. This place might seem weird, but Japan is the home of keirin.' Sam looked at Mitch as if he was mad. But, since he always seemed to know everything, Sam presumed he probably knew what he was talking about. Mitch carried on: 'You know how, in England, football is the biggest, most important sport, yeah?' Sam nodded. 'Well, it's different in different countries. In New Zealand it's rugby they like best. In Canada it's ice hockey. In Finland they love ski-jumping and javelin. Don't ask me why . . . I know, Finland sounds weird. And here in Japan they're in love with sumo wrestling and keirin.'

Still, Sam looked at Mitch as if he didn't believe him.

'Look, Sam,' Mitch said, 'keirin here is like a religion and the best keirin riders are like gods. They're paid like gods too. Being a keirin superstar here is like being Wayne Rooney back home. You get silly money. Really brilliantly silly money.'

On that note, Sam decided that it wasn't such a bad place and he walked into class feeling that maybe it was worth it after all. Plus, he also knew that there was one rule here that he really liked: to graduate from Keirin School the Japanese boys had to study there for nine months, yet the foreign recruits like Mitch and himself only had to do two weeks.

And so for two weeks Sam and Mitch sat in class hearing about bikes, riding technique and how to take your bike apart and then put it back together again. Everything that the teachers said was translated into English, and Sam and Mitch would write it down. And they knew that if they didn't pass at the end of the fortnight they wouldn't get to compete on the Japanese Keirin Grand Prix circuit and would be sent straight home.

Actually, being sent home often seemed a better idea than staying and sharing your bedroom with a family of cockroaches. But as the days passed, and they got used to the cockroaches and the robes and the early morning alarm, it didn't seem quite so bad. And anyway, Sam had become intrigued by a boy called Chen.

The best part of Keirin School was every afternoon when they finally got out of class and on to their bikes. The school didn't just have one velodrome, it had four. And all four velodromes sat perched high on the top of a hill, peeking out of a ring of clouds. They looked magical. From his desk in the classroom, Sam could see out of the window and up the hill and he'd look longingly up at those four velodromes every morning, staring at them as if he was gazing up at heaven.

And in the afternoons, when they got to one of the velodromes, he'd watch Chen. Chen was the best bike-rider Sam had ever seen.

Every day, they'd warm up on the track, lap after lap, this huge crowd of riders going round and round as if they were in a traffic jam going to work. And then they'd stop and individually they'd be timed: how fast can you do one kilometre on your own? And every day Chen would win.

Sam thought that was pretty impressive, but what impressed him even more was when they got down to the serious business: the keirin racing. Sam started watching Chen closely, studying his moves, observing how he raced. The first time he watched him, Sam saw how Chen stayed at the back of the pack all the way and then only made his break to the front on the last lap. In the next race he did completely the opposite: he was at the front from the beginning and was so powerful he didn't allow anyone else to overtake. And the third time he stayed near the front, glued himself to the wheel of the leader and drafted all the way until, with half a lap to go, he pulled out, overtook and sprinted for the line.

Amazing. Most people only knew one way to win. Sam certainly did: he had to draft near the front, otherwise he had no chance. But Chen had three different ways of winning a race and every one of them worked. And here he was practising all three methods every day.

It was not until after a week that Sam was put in the same race as Chen. As they waited to go on the track, Sam said, '*Konnichiwa*,' to Chen, but the boy just looked away, as if he was embarrassed. Sam didn't mind. He was far more interested in seeing whether he could beat Chen by drafting on the back of his wheel.

Minutes later, Sam, Chen and four others were on the track, following the derney. Everyone scrambled for the place they wanted; it was a bit messy, but, the moment the derny pulled off, Sam made sure he was behind Chen. He was determined to hang on from there and it seemed to be working fine. But then Chen slowed down so Sam did too. He didn't want to, but had no choice. And, Chen kept on slowing, so much so that he was right at the back of the pack. And if Chen was at the back of the pack, it meant that Sam was even further behind.

Sam felt uneasy. He waited for Chen to make his move. He had to, didn't he? He couldn't stay there, right at the back. Sam waited and waited and Chen just did nothing. They passed the lap-to-go mark and still Chen didn't move.

Right, thought Sam, *time for Plan B. I'm going. Chen can stay here if he wants, but I'm not going to.* And so he yanked his handlebar to the right, swerved out and thundered down on the pedals, accelerating smoothly past Chen and off to the front. But the split second that Sam had passed him Chen followed. Suddenly, having followed Chen's wheel for the entire race, Chen was now glued to his. Sam flicked a look back; Chen seemed to know exactly what he was doing.

With one bend to go, Sam decided to go for glory. He cycled even harder, edging his way bit by bit to the front. Finally, he had his wheel ahead. But Chen was right behind him. Sam had done all the work and he'd taken Chen with him. And then Chen tugged gently on his handlebars, veered out and suddenly he was alongside Sam. And when they hit the line he had zipped ahead.

Sam leaned forward in the saddle, gasping for breath. He couldn't believe it. His plan had been to draft off the back of Chen, but instead Chen had drafted off the back of him. That was so completely annoying. And Chen had been brilliant. He had completely and utterly outwitted him.

As Sam sucked in breath after breath, trying to recover, he wheeled round the track and eventually pulled up alongside Chen. And, as they rolled along together, he put out a hand and Chen shook it.

Then Sam tried again. '*Konnichiwa*,' he said. '*Konnichiwa!*' But again Chen looked away, then he cycled off and was gone. That was strange and Sam wondered why Chen wouldn't talk to him.

At school every day after that, Sam would try to bump into Chen and say, '*Konnichiwa*,' but he never got a reply. Chen would just look a little embarrassed, as if he was flustered and didn't know how to say hello back. But, as Sam watched him, he realized that actually Chen didn't say '*Konnichiwa*' to anyone. In fact, Chen kept himself completely to himself. So Sam pretty much gave up. If Chen didn't want to be friendly, it didn't bother him. Anyway, it was the last day of Keirin School and he had his exam to pass.

After all the hours he'd spent with Mr Parrott and the Professor, tinkering with bikes and bike parts, Sam felt confident that he'd pass the exam. It was simple: you had to take your bike apart completely, so that every little component had been taken off it. Then you had to shout, '*Owarimasu!*' which meant 'Finished'. And then you had to put the bike together again and shout, '*Owarimasu!*' once more. And you had to do it all in less than twenty minutes.

'Is this going to help me in the Olympics, Mitch?' Sam asked. He was still convinced that Keirin School was weird.

'No,' Mitch replied, 'but it might help you make lots of money on the Grand Prix circuit.'

'OK,' said Sam. 'Bring it on.'

A buzzer then sounded to indicate that the exam had started and Sam and Mitch got to work. Sam worked away confidently. Mr Parrott had been an excellent teacher so he knew exactly what he was doing. He didn't rush; he just worked sensibly, dismantling and then rebuilding. After sixteen minutes, he shouted, '*Owarimasu!*' for the second time. He was then told he could wait outside the classroom. He had passed.

Outside was one other boy: It seemed no surprise that the one person who had beaten him was Chen.

'*Konnichiwa!*' Sam said again. He didn't expect to get a word back, but this time Chen finally spoke. He didn't say, '*Konnichiwa!*' Instead he said, 'China!' Then he pointed at himself and said it again: 'China. Chen, China.'

Sam stared at him as if he was trying to understand some kind of a riddle. And then it clicked. 'I get it, I get it,' he said. 'You're Chinese! Not Japanese!' Chen nodded his head furiously, smiling from ear to ear.

'I see!' Sam said, all his thoughts tumbling out together. 'I'd just assumed that you were Japanese like everyone else. How dumb of me. Does that mean that you're competing on the Grand Prix circuit with Mitch and me?'

Chen shrugged. He looked completely confused.

'Oh yes, sorry,' Sam said. 'It's not very helpful if I speak in English, is it? Hang on . . .' He paused and thought for a second, trying to recall 'hello' in Mandarin. Remembering, he then said, '*Ni hao!*'

Chen's eyes lit up. He thought that was very funny. '*Ni hao!*' he said back.

Sam paused to think again, and then, slowly, feeling a little embarrassed, he asked a question that he could remember from his Mandarin lessons at school: '*Ni shi cong nar lai de?*' – 'Where are you from?'

Chen really liked that; just hearing Sam say it seemed to bring a big smile to his face. Then Chen replied, 'Shanghai,' and nodded, as if he was waiting for Sam to ask another question.

And so Sam asked the next thing he could remember from his Mandarin lessons: 'How old are you?' And then: 'Do you have any brothers and sisters?' And, as he got more confident, he started to ask questions in Mandarin that hadn't come straight from the textbooks. He asked, 'Are you going to come to the London Olympics?'

Chen paused and then answered. Sam wasn't completely sure he understood the answer because Chen spoke so fast, but he thought he said, 'I do not know. I hope so. It is very hard to get into the China team.'

And then Sam thought of another question which he was really pleased with: 'How come you are so fast?' But Chen didn't answer that; he just giggled so hard he could hardly stop. Sam liked that.

★ 17 ★

KARATE ON WHEELS

Sam knew that keirin racing in Japan would be different from anything he had come across before, and that was before someone slapped him in the face in the middle of a race.

In fact, for their first race, he and Mitch were so amazed by the whole scene, they were more like tourists than riders trying to win. And Sam stayed that way, even after the slap.

He and Mitch were to compete in four keirin Grand Prix events before they returned home. That meant four events in four different major cities, each of them four days apart. In their lessons at Keirin School, they'd been warned that the Japanese crowd tended to go a little bit crazy, but nothing had prepared them for this.

Their first Grand Prix was in Hiroshima. They were picked up at the airport and driven to the velodrome and, as they approached, they could hear a strange, high-pitched screaming. It was the fans. They were outside the gates with their faces pushed up against the wire fence, and they were shouting, so excited, so loud, and they didn't stop. And that was outside the velodrome; inside they were even louder.

Inside something else rather strange happened. In the changing rooms beneath the track, where they could hear the shouts and screams of the crowd above, Sam and Mitch were each given a zipped-up bag, which contained a whole load of protective clothing. It was the kind of equipment that you wear to play American football, not what you put on for a bike ride. There was protection for the arms, the shoulders and the hands, a helmet for the head of course, and, weirdest of all, a big vest with a carbon-fibre plate in it to protect the spine. When they put everything on, they were so padded they felt more like astronauts than cyclists. As soon as they started racing, though, everything finally became clear. Keirin racing in Japan was extremely violent – more violent than anything Sam had watched on YouTube.

In Mitch's first race, the moment the derny pulled away, the rider on Mitch's right leaned into him, trying to shove him out of the way with his elbow. However, having been forced away from him, Mitch went bang into the rider on his left. He then got shoved back the other way. So his first ride was not about winning the race, it was about trying not to fall off. He finished last, but was happy just to stay alive.

In Sam's first race he was doing quite well. At least, so he thought. With 200 metres to go, he was winning. He wondered how much money he might get. All he had to do was outpower the rider who was trying to overtake him on his right. With 100 metres to go, he looked over his right shoulder to see where the rival rider was and at him, the very moment he looked the rider whacked him with an open-hand smack in the face. Wow, did that hurt! It stung so much that his eyes watered and he lost control of the bike and nearly fell off. By the time he regained control of it, the rider who'd hit him was way ahead. And so was everyone else. So he finished last too. And, like Mitch, he just felt lucky to be alive.

'It's not bike-racing,' said Sam. 'It's like a fight on wheels.'

'It's like a karate contest at forty miles an hour,' Mitch said.

'It's like having a boxing match on a roller-coaster,' said Sam.

'It's just crazy,' Mitch said. 'So come on – let's do it again!'

In keirin racing in the Olympics the rules are very strict. You cannot barge or shove anyone; in fact, you're barely allowed to touch them. Here, though, it was all different.

The only person who seemed unaffected by it all was Chen. His race was after Sam's and Sam decided to watch him. He already watched almost everything that Chen did on a bike; he was just so good it seemed there was always something Sam could learn from him.

Sure enough, Chen's race turned out to be another lesson. He didn't get barged or shoved by anyone, or smacked in the face; in fact, he managed to steer almost completely clear of this new game of 'karate on wheels'. Instead, he just pulled off one of the strategies that Sam had seen from him at Keirin School: he stayed at the back, right out of trouble where no one could hurt him. And then, with 150 metres to go, he suddenly put his foot down, as if an electric charge was suddenly shooting through his legs, and he burst to the front. And no, it wasn't completely simple. Just as he was getting to the front, one of the riders stretched out his right arm to try to stop him, but Chen was so powerful he just brushed past him. He was awesome.

Afterwards, Sam tried to congratulate Chen, but Chen seemed distracted and deep in conversation with a man on the side of the track. And then Chen immediately left and made a long phone call. He seemed very serious, very stressed.

So Sam left him to it, and he and Mitch got ready for their next races. But second time around, they didn't go much better either.

Mitch thought he was doing well until his handlebars got clattered as he was overtaking on the outside; he lost his balance, nearly fell off and finished last again. Sam decided to copy Chen's tactics and stay at the back and out of trouble. But, when they got to 150 metres from the finish, he found he simply didn't have as much power as Chen to launch himself to the front. So he finished third last.

They then watched Chen's next race and again he was brilliant. This time he used another of the tactics that Sam had seen at Keirin School. He avoided all the karate action by starting right at the front, staying there and refusing to let anyone get close enough to threaten him. So that was another impressive victory for him; Sam and Mitch were finished for the day, but Chen was in the final.

Again Sam and Mitch went to congratulate him, but again he was distracted. Even when he wasn't talking to the man in the stands, he seemed too busy to talk to them.

'Maybe he's just like this when he's competing,' said Mitch.

'You're probably right,' Sam answered. 'But it's still a little weird. Back at Keirin School he was our mate.'

'He still is our mate,' Mitch said. 'Come on. Let's go and watch his final. Do you know what the prize money is for the winner?'

'No.'

Mitch chuckled to himself. 'Around twenty thousand pounds. Seriously.'

In the race, Chen was as good as ever. In fact, Sam thought he was even better. He deployed his third tactic this time, which involved racing from right in the middle of the pack, right in the thick of the karate on wheels, and, as soon as the derny pulled off, he went straight on to the back of the wheel of the leading rider and stuck to it like glue.

Sam watched carefully. There was quite a lot of shoving, but Chen didn't seem bothered by it. He simply ignored it. And he remained on the wheel of the leading rider until he approached the final bend and then, bang, he was up and away, overtaking him so fast it was as if he was turbocharged. As Chen went through the finishing line, he was a metre clear of everyone else and the crowd were screaming louder than they had done all day. He raised his hands in victory, punching the air in delight, still flying round the track but with no hands on the handlebars. Sam and Mitch were thrilled for him.

Afterwards, Chen had to receive a medal and his cheque and shake lots of hands, but Sam and Mitch waited for him in the changing room. They wanted to congratulate him and by the time they got to see him the fans had all gone home; most of the other riders had left too and the velodrome seemed strangely quiet.

When Chen came down to the changing room, he was with the same man he'd been talking to in the stands. The man wore a tight-fitting tracksuit jacket and he didn't come in; he just hung around the doorway as if he was waiting for Chen who sat down and started taking off his shoes.

'Well done, Chen,' Sam said in his best Mandarin. 'We are so pleased for you.'

Chen nodded and, quietly, said, '*Xie xie*,' Mandarin for 'thank you'. But he kept looking down at his feet. He didn't look at Sam or Mitch at all.

Mitch couldn't speak Mandarin, but he wasn't going to hold back, even though he knew that Chen wouldn't understand a word. 'You're a complete diamond,' he said in English. 'The crowd out there loved you!' And he patted Chen on the shoulder, but, as he did so, he could feel Chen's muscles tensing, as if he didn't want to be touched.

Mitch looked at Sam and shrugged his shoulders. This all felt a bit strange. Sam translated Mitch's words. 'Mitch says he thinks you are a diamond,' Sam said, trying his hardest to speak his best Mandarin. Chen looked up very quickly and flashed him an uncertain smile then carried on getting changed. 'In England,' Sam said to him, 'if you are a diamond, it means you are rare and precious. So it means you are very, very good.'

Still Chen didn't reply. He looked up for a moment at the man waiting in the doorway, but not at Sam or Mitch. So Sam decided to have one more go. He thought hard. He was searching for a really good sentence in Mandarin. And then he said, 'Chen, your tactics were brilliant today. If you ride like that in the London Olympics, no one can possibly catch you.'

But it was the same. No reply, nothing. Chen took off his riding gloves and looked down at his hands, though he did flash another look at the man in the tracksuit jacket. There was an awkward silence in the room. Sam and Mitch looked at each other and then at the same time they said, 'Come on, time to go.'

★ 18 ★

CHINA CRISIS

After Hiroshima, the keirin circus moved on to Tokyo, Japan's capital city. Then they would go to Kyoto and, before going back to England, Sam and Mitch would ride their final keirin races in Osaka.

Tokyo was an extraordinary city. Sam and Mitch went for a little walk and were amazed by the lights and high buildings and the huge advertising hoardings. It felt massive, bigger than London. And, because they couldn't read the Japanese alphabet, they couldn't decipher the road signs, and pretty soon they were lost and had to get a taxi back to the hotel where they were staying. And that was the end of sightseeing. They were not there to be tourists; they were there to try to learn how to win this sport of karate on wheels.

'We've got to be more physical,' said Mitch.

'What do you mean?'

'Well, we both got pushed around so much last time, we had no chance. We have to be prepared for it. And, instead of just being shoved around the whole time by the other riders, we have to try to push them back.'

Three days later, Sam was on the startline in the Tokyo velodrome. He felt strong and confident, and that was mainly because he had Mitch's words buzzing round in his head. 'Come on,' he said to himself. 'Don't let them push you around.' But that was easier said than done.

When the race started, Sam got himself in a good position. He was in third place, drafting beautifully and waiting patiently for the derny to pull aside, at which point the race would come alive. The moment the derny moved though – whack! – he got an elbow in his ribs from the rider to the inside of him. Sam felt it and it hurt, but he didn't even look back. *Don't be pushed around*, was the thought in his head. *Don't be pushed around!*

And then, just as they were approaching the bend, Sam decided it was time to join in. He waited until the other rider was right next to him, and then he thrust out his left elbow, straight into the other man's ribs. The rider wobbled a bit and fell behind. *Brilliant*, Sam thought to himself. *That'll show him.*

But it didn't. All it did was make him angry. Sam pedalled on, riding hard, but he made one massive mistake: he failed to notice that the rider he was in a private battle with had come up alongside him again. *Oh dear. Never lose your concentration.*

Because, the moment Sam looked away, the rider on his left whacked him back again and this time Sam lost balance badly and swung over to his right. And just as he swung right, the rider on his right-hand side sped past him, knocking his front wheel inwards.

No rider would have survived this. It was like trying to turn right while your handlebars were turning left. And it happened so quickly Sam could do nothing. It just felt horrifying, a total lack of control, his bicycle slipping away from underneath him as if someone had rugby-tackled it, and then he fell hard, really, really hard, and clattered on to the track.

His right hip hit the ground first, the pain surging through his body. Then his shoulder whacked down on to the ground and then his head. Thank God for the helmet. It probably saved his life. And then he slid. And when you fall off a bike at forty-two miles per hour, it's not just the fall that hurts because you don't come to an immediate halt. You're going so fast that you skid along the ground and your skin scrapes along the track and it feels as though someone is rubbing you hard with sandpaper.

When he finally ground to a halt, Sam's race was over and he was wailing with the pain. He stood up and looked at his thigh – his clothing had torn and under the shredded material he could see that his skin had rubbed away too and he was red and bloody. It stung so much.

That was his day over. He was too injured to race again. He went straight off to have his wounds looked at by a doctor so he didn't see Mitch, who did quite well, and finished second twice. And he didn't see Chen who again won every race.

The following week they were in Kyoto and Sam's injuries had healed enough for him to be able to race again. And he did better. He actually won his first race and finished second in the next one. Mitch did well too and both of them qualified for the final. But Chen won the final. He had still not lost a race. And he had now won over £50,000.

Afterwards, Sam and Mitch were really excited. They felt they were finally learning how to win. And, in their excitement, they tried to talk to Chen, but he again gave them the cold shoulder. It was strange; only three weeks ago they'd all become friends at Keirin School, but now Chen was acting as if he didn't know them. And that man, the one who always wore a zipped-up tracksuit top, seemed to follow Chen everywhere. He wouldn't let him out of his sight.

So Sam and Mitch travelled on to Osaka, their last event, and they tried to forget about Chen. Sam was just desperate to do well there so he could go home with some good news for the Professor and Mr Parrott and Grandad and his mum. He wanted them to be proud of him. So far, all he had to show for his long stay in Japan was a single victory in Kyoto and a long red wound along his right hip.

So, thank goodness, Osaka went well – really well – for both Sam and Mitch. And Chen. But then it always went well for Chen.

Sam really felt he was learning. He was getting the hang of how to handle all the pushing and shoving, and he also knew what he had to do to win. It was now absolutely clear to him that he wasn't as good as Chen and he didn't have three different strategies. He only had one, but he knew that if he got it right, then he had a good chance.

He had to be the best, smartest drafter in the race. He had to use all the skills he'd learned from his newspaper run, from following that red Honda Civic and all those other cars, because only that way could he give himself a chance of doing well.

So, in his first race, he glued himself to the back wheel of the leader and stayed there until 125 metres to go. Then he pulled out and, feeling he still had enough energy left, he hammered down on the pedals, edged forward and, when they hit the line, he was centimetres ahead.

In his second race, it wasn't so simple. He tried to glue himself to the front rider, but he pulled aside and suddenly he was at the front instead. But the front rider knew he wasn't strong enough to win that way, so he pulled aside too and immediately slotted back into the pack and locked himself on to the back wheel of the rider who'd taken the lead. That was good and he felt pleased. He stayed there and then, at exactly the same place, with 125 metres to go, he pulled out, hammered down on the pedals again and edged to the front.

That was two victories out of two. An hour later, he sat motionless on his saddle waiting for his last race in Japan. The final. On his left was Mitch, who had also qualified. And on his right was Chen, who had still not yet lost a race.

The race started and as they followed the derny, Sam looked around. Mitch was close by him and Chen was right at the back. Then the derny pulled away and they were immediately racing and the pushing and shoving started. But Sam was determined not to be shaken by the karate on wheels.

'Be strong,' he said to himself. 'Don't get pushed. Don't start pushing the others. Just glue yourself on to the wheel of the leader.'

Sure enough, the race started going to plan. He locked on to the leader's wheel. He was centimetres off it, drafting perfectly – waiting, waiting, waiting for the right moment. And then, same as before, with 125 metres to go, he pulled out, hammered down on the pedals and started edging ahead. As he went, the noise of the crowd seemed to fade, going from loud to nothing, and he was so focused on powering his bike forward he couldn't hear anything.

They zipped round the final bend at nearly forty-five miles per hour. Sam was just in the lead – he only had to hold on. But then he felt another bike on his right shoulder. It was Mitch. Him and Mitch, best friend versus best friend, a head-to-head sprint for the line. The final few seconds were a blur. Sam and Mitch charged through the line and then both flopped over their handlebars, coasting round the arena, exhausted.

'Who won it?' Sam shouted out to Mitch.

'I don't know!' Mitch shouted back. They could barely hear themselves above the screams and yells of the crowd.

So they stopped and watched the replay on the big screen. They saw Sam ahead, they saw Mitch edging slowly closer, and then they saw something else that neither of them was aware of at the time. While they'd been engaged in their head-to-head, Chen had been chasing them furiously on the outside. So Sam got beaten by Mitch, by a couple of centimetres, but Mitch didn't win the race either. Chen did. He beat them both easily. Chen was awesome.

That night Sam and Mitch went out for a meal together. They'd been beaten by Chen, but they still felt that they'd done well and they were happy. It helped that they'd been given some prize money too. Sam had won £5,000 and he knew exactly what he was going to do with it.

But they were also tired, completely exhausted, and so they went back to their hotel to get an early night before their flight home the next day. And there, at the hotel, a surprise was waiting for them. It was Chen. And he was on his own; the man in the tracksuit top was nowhere to be seen.

Chen looked nervous. He kept looking around, as if he didn't want to be seen. 'Can we talk?' he asked.

Sam nodded and they went quickly upstairs to Sam and Mitch's room. When the door closed behind them, Chen didn't even sit down, he just started talking loud and fast, so fast that Sam couldn't understand a word he was saying.

'Slow down,' Sam said in Mandarin, waving his hands to try and explain that he didn't understand what Chen was saying. 'Why don't you sit down first?'

So Chen sat down. It was strange but after winning today, his fourth time in a row, he seemed sad. He spoke slowly, so that Sam could understand, and he kept looking away from Sam and Mitch, as if he was embarrassed.

'I just wanted to say sorry,' he said.

'Why?' Sam asked.

'Because you are my friends. I have never before talked to anyone who is not Chinese. So, at the beginning, I was scared of you two. But you were so friendly. You talked to me in my language. I like you. You are my friends.'

Mitch and Sam nodded back to him. 'You are our friend too, Chen,' Sam said.

Chen then explained that, in China, it is very important that he always wins every race. He said that when he was ten, because he was so good at bike-racing, he was taken away from home and sent to a school hundreds of miles away so that he could train every day to be an Olympic cyclist. This wasn't his choice or his parents' either, he explained. But he was told that, if he did well, his family could have a nicer house in Shanghai.

'Well, with all that prize money you have won here in Japan,' Sam said, 'you can buy them an even nicer house now.'

'No,' Chen said. 'You do not understand. It does not work like that. I am not even allowed to keep the money.'

'What?' Sam couldn't believe what he was hearing. He translated everything back to Mitch so that he could understand too. Sam then asked, 'Why? Why not? It is your money.'

Chen paused and then explained. 'In my country, the government says that because it has paid for my education and my training as a cyclist it kind of owns me. So, if I win money, it belongs to my government. I have already had my money taken off me.'

'Who by?' Sam asked. 'That man in the tracksuit?'

'Yes,' Chen said.

'Who is he?'

'He is my coach. But he is more than a coach. He is like a police officer. He did not want me to talk to you. In Hiroshima and Kyoto, why did I not speak to you? Because you are not my friends? No. Because he was standing there.'

'But I don't understand, what is wrong with you talking to us?' Sam asked.

'He says it is not good to be friends with people who are my enemies on the track.'

Sam shook his head in dismay. 'But what could he have done?'

'He could make big trouble for me. He could take away my house and my car. He could tell me that I will no longer be a cyclist for China, that I will not go to the Olympics.' Chen paused as Sam translated for Mitch. 'I am a bit scared of my coach,' he said. 'He does not know that I have come here to see you. If he did, he would be furious. And I would be in trouble. I said to him tonight: "Goodnight, I am very tired, I am going to bed." And then an hour later I had to creep out. I was scared that he would see me.'

'It sounds like he should defect,' Mitch said to Sam. He was only joking really, but Sam translated it anyway and Chen looked surprised.

Sam and Mitch looked at each other with concern

in their eyes. 'What can we do?' Mitch said to Sam. 'Ask Chen if there's anything we can do.'

But Chen shook his head. 'No, there is nothing you can do. All I ask is that you are still my friends,' he said. 'I wanted you to understand why I did not talk to you. I wanted to talk to you, but I could not.'

'We understand,' Sam said. 'And you are our fricnd too.'

Mitch said to Sam, 'Ask him if he has an email address.'

He did and so they all exchanged addresses. Then Mitch had another idea: 'Sam, ask him if we're allowed to be Facebook friends.'

'Nice idea, but too dangerous, I think,' Chen said. He looked at his watch. 'And I must go,' he added. 'I have been away too long. But thank you, Sam, and thank you, Mitch. Thank you for being my friends.'

And with that he was out of the door and gone.

★ 19 ★

BUSINESS PARTNERS

It was great to be back in England. When Sam got home, one of the first things he did was to call round to Anything & Everything. He knew Mr Parrott would be desperate to hear how Japan had gone.

Mr Parrott said nothing for about twenty minutes as Sam told him the whole story – about Keirin School, about karate on wheels and about his new friend, the sad but brilliantly talented Chen. Sam thought that this was probably the longest that Mr Parrott had been silent ever since he'd known him.

At the end of the conversation, Sam had one more big surprise for him. He fished around in his back pocket and pulled out a cheque for £5,000.

'Here,' he said, 'why don't we spend this together?'

'What do you mean?' Mr Parrott said, surprised.

'Well, I'm so grateful to you for all the help you've given me. I'd never have become a cyclist without you. So I thought it was about time I helped you back. I know what you've always really, really wanted and that's to run a bike shop. With some of my winnings, maybe you could start to sell anything and everything and a few bikes too.'

Mr Parrott looked at Sam in disbelief. He could hardly talk. 'Well, er, well, Sam, I don't know, I don't know what to say. It's your money, not mine. I couldn't possibly take it.'

'What if we think of it as a kind of loan?'

'How do you mean?'

'Well, I can't do your newspaper round any more. I've got to move to Manchester to live in a flat with Mitch and some of the other British cyclists. And it strikes me that there must be easier ways of making money. Why don't you just start selling a few bikes, kids' bikes, and offering to mend them? And on my days off I can come and work for you. Keirin School taught me enough about mending bikes to solve any problem. Let's just start by doing that. And if, one day, it takes off, you can upgrade and start selling Giant bikes like mine.'

Mr Parrott still seemed lost for words. Sam could see that the vein on the side of his head had started to bulge again. He chuckled to himself; he thought the vein only bulged when Mr Parrott was cross, but maybe it bulged when he was happy too.

'What about the money, Sam?' he asked.

'Oh, easy,' Sam said. 'You know when you bought me my Giant? And I paid you back bit by bit? Well, why don't we do the same? As you start to make money off your bike business, you can pay it back in instalments.'

Mr Parrott now had tears in his eyes. 'Sam,' he said. 'You're one special kid. I accept your offer.' He stuck out his hand and Sam shook it firmly. They had a deal.

★ 20 ★

THE SECRET SQUIRREL CLUB

There were now less than ten months until the London Olympics and the atmosphere at the Manchester velodrome had got very serious.

Life for Mitch and Sam got serious too. They'd been back in Manchester for a month when they received a message: the Professor wanted to see them in his office. They'd never been in it before. If you were summoned there, the news was either very good or exceedingly bad.

It turned out that his office was far from normal. It had a desk and a computer and a phone like most offices do, but it was more like a cross between a workshop and a science laboratory. There were bicycle parts lying around on the floor and hanging up on the walls. There were bike helmets of different shapes and sizes all lined up in a row – twelve of them, Sam counted. There were twenty wheels, all lined up together. There were rows of bike shoes, bike pedals, bike saddles, saddle posts. Everything to do with a bike was in there. It felt like a bike factory.

And, intriguingly, there was a door in the corner with a massive padlock on it.

'Welcome,' said the Professor, 'to the Secret Squirrel Club.'

Sam and Mitch looked at each other. 'The Secret Squirrel Club?' said Sam.

'The Secret Squirrel Club,' the Professor explained, 'is where we try to be ingenious.' He looked at Sam. 'Like you, Sam, in the Junior National Champs, when you had to do some smar thinking to mend your bike. Well, we're trying to do that here. I don't think we're doing too bad a job of it either.'

'What do you mean?' Mitch asked.

'Well, I can't tell you, can I?' the Professor said, laughing. 'It's secret!'

Sam and Mitch shrugged. They didn't understand.

'OK,' the Professor started to explain. 'If we're going to win the Olympics, we need the best riders in the world, don't we? But we need something else too. We need the best bikes, the best helmets, the best kit, the best everything. We need anything we can find to help us go faster. This is what I really enjoy doing: sitting in here, in the Secret Squirrel Club, trying to invent the fastest equipment in the world.'

'Like the Flying Scotsman!' Sam said who thought this was brilliant. 'Are you going to use parts of a washing machine?'

The Professor laughed. 'I might do. I couldn't possibly say.'

'So what have you invented?' Sam asked. 'What's the secret?'

The Professor shook his head and laughed heartily again. 'If you think I'm going to tell you that, you must be mad! It's one thing to tell you that there's a Secret Squirrel Club, it's quite another to tell you what the Secret Squirrel Club has invented. Everything we've done is behind there –' he pointed to the padlocked door '– and Mac and I are the only people in the world with a key to it!'

Sam and Mitch stared at the door. What on earth was behind it?

'So is Mac in your Secret Squirrel Club?' Sam asked. He tried not to sound too surprised.

'He sure is,' the Professor said. 'He might not be the most charming of coaches, but he has a bright mind. When I have a crazy new idea, I often invite Mac down to tell me if it's good or simply bonkers.'

But then Mitch piped up. 'I've got a question.'

'Go ahead.'

'Why are you telling us about all this stuff for the London Olympics? We're too young to compete.'

'Ah yes, good point,' he replied. 'Actually, I don't think you're too young at all. I've been watching you both very closely since you came back from Japan and I'm very impressed with what I've seen. You're both being promoted. You're both now going up into the

Great Britain senior squad. It's going to be hard. Very, very hard. The senior squad are extremely strong indeed. But so are you two. You've become exceedingly good keirin riders. As things stand, Mitch, I think you're probably the number one keirin rider in the country. And you, Sam, I'd say that you're probably number two. We can only have one rider in each event, but if you two work hard enough I'd be very surprised if I don't see one of you competing in the London Olympics.'

★ 21 ★

HOW TO DO A DALEY THOMPSON

The Olympics! Sam could not believe that he really had a chance of going to the London Olympics. Ever since Grandad had told him the story about his great-grandfather and the 1940 Helsinki Olympics that never happened, Sam had dreamed of competing in the Games. He so wanted to do it – for himself, for his mother, for Grandad and for his great-grandfather too. But he'd never even considered London. He'd always assumed he'd be too young to compete. However, the more he thought about it, the more London seemed a better and better idea. If he got to the London Games, then Grandad could come and watch.

Sam went away from the Secret Squirrel Club with the Professor's words spinning round his head: '*If you work hard enough, you could compete in the Games.*' If. Why *if*? If there was the remotest chance of getting to ride in the London Olympics, then Sam was determined to grab it. If? There was no *if*. Not to Sam.

Over the next few months, he trained harder than he'd ever done in his life. Did he go to watch City? No chance, he didn't have time. City were flying high, but all Sam could do was watch them on *Match of the Day*. Because Sam wanted to fly high too.

Every week he'd work two afternoons for Mr Parrott. He liked it. Mr Parrott would ask so many questions: he wanted to know what Sam was doing in training, what he was eating, what the Professor was like, what kind of exercises he was doing in the gym. Sam told him everything and Mr Parrott was fascinated.

One day, when Sam told him about the Secret Squirrel Club, Mr Parrott was so excited that he spilled his cup of tea down his shirt. Sam wondered if maybe this was the most exciting thing Mr Parrott had ever heard in his life.

'What do you think they've got behind that locked door?' he asked. And though Sam didn't have the answer, he thought a lot about that too. On those two days when he was mending broken bikes for Mr Parrott, his mind would drift to the room in the velodrome where the Secret Squirrel Club was based and it would settle on that locked door. He was desperate to know what was behind it.

But there was just one problem though with training hard: Mitch was too. There was only one rider Sam had ever met who could work harder than him and endure more pain than him – and that was Mitch.

It was tough because Mitch was his mate. They always trained together and Mitch would encourage him. 'Come on, Sam,' he'd say. 'Good work, Sam!'

Yet Mitch was so good, so talented. Sam was too – he was very good – but he knew deep down that Mitch was marginally better. It felt strange: Mitch was Sam's friend, yet every day Sam was desperate to beat him. He almost became the enemy. But how could you be enemies with someone who encourages you so much? And Sam couldn't help but wonder, every day in training, if he'd ever overtake him.

Soon Sam started doing extra training. At the velodrome they'd train from Monday to Saturday and have Sunday off. But Sam decided to train on Sundays too. And when they were given a one-hour weights session in the gym, Sam would do one hour and fifteen minutes. He did everything he could possibly think of to catch up with Mitch. And when he'd run out of ideas, he'd talk to Mr Parrott about it.

'Have you thought about doing a Daley Thompson?' Mr Parrott suggested. And he explained to Sam that Daley Thompson had been one of the best British track and field athletes of all time. Maybe the very best. In the Olympics, Mr Parrot explained, the hardest athletics event to win is the decathlon. And Daley Thompson won the gold medal in the Moscow Olympics in 1980 and then he won it again in 1984.

And everyone remembers when he was given his gold medal in 1984, Mr Parrott said, because when they played 'God Save the Queen' Daley stood on the podium and whistled the tune.

But the thing about Daley Thompson, Mr Parrott went on, was that he would do anything to have the edge over the opposition. So he decided that he'd train on Christmas Day. When all the other athletes were going to be at home with their families, taking a rare day off and eating turkey and stuffing, Thompson went out and trained hard.

'Right,' Sam said. 'When Christmas Day comes, I'm going to be out there too.'

★ 22 ★

CHRISTMAS PRESENTS

Christmas Day was cold. There was a slight frost, a bit of early morning ice on the roads, but that didn't put Sam off. While most kids were still opening their stockings, he was already out on the road.

He set off on a familiar path, past Garrold Street, Arthur Road and Eric Avenue, up Freshton Hill, through Twizzlebury and Reakton, the old places that he used to come to every day with a trailer full of newspapers dragging behind him. This time, though, he skipped up Freshton Hill as if it was barely a bump in the road. His legs felt good, the air was sparkling and fresh in his lungs and he loved the thought that was going through his head: *I'm doing a Daley! I'm doing a Daley!*

From Reakton he turned right and headed up towards the hills of the Peak District. It was beautiful out on the road with barely a single car out there for company. Everyone else would be tucked up warm and cosy for Christmas.

As he neared the climb to the Winnats Pass, he

still felt strong. The only thing that bothered him was the sight, in the far distance, of another cyclist on the road, coming towards him. The cyclist had a good technique and the closer he got, the more familiar he looked. And then in no time, there, right in front of him, was Mitch.

Sam couldn't believe it. He pulled on the brakes and stopped, and Mitch did the same, and they both burst out laughing.

'Do you know who Daley Thompson is?' Sam asked.

'I certainly do,' Mitch replied. 'If it wasn't for Daley Thompson, we'd probably both be about to tuck into Christmas lunch by now.'

'Happy Christmas, Mitch!' Sam said.

'Happy Christmas to you too,' Mitch replied. 'Do you fancy riding together?'

'Why not.' So Mitch turned his bike round and they headed back up the Winnats Pass, laughing to each other as they went.

'What do you want for Christmas?' Mitch asked.

'A key to the padlocked door of the Secret Squirrel Club!' Sam said, laughing. 'What about you?'

Mitch paused and thought about it. 'A pair of legs that are faster than Chen's.'

Sam laughed and then accelerated ahead up the road, shouting, 'You've got to get past me first, mate!'

Mitch set off in hot pursuit and they found

themselves racing each other up the Winnats Pass, pushing harder and harder the higher the road climbed. At the top they stopped and shook hands.

'It's going to be a hard year for us, Sam,' Mitch said. 'But good luck to you. You're a great rider.'

'Good luck to you too,' Sam said. 'You're a good mate.'

After the Winnats Pass, they decided to ride together for another two hours, taking turns to lead, and when the road was empty they cycled side by side, chatting eagerly about what the year ahead had in store for them. One of them, surely, was going to compete in the London Olympic Games.

Towards the end, when they were getting tired, Sam took up the lead with Mitch glued to his wheel. They headed towards Buxton, down a slight hill, past a dairy farm and into a shaded right-hand bend. And there and then, suddenly, the joy of the day, the joy of Christmas, the joy of the Olympics exploded.

Sam took the bend and Mitch tried to follow his line. But he hadn't seen that there was still frost on the road. His bike slipped, he tried to rebalance, but he was too close to Sam.

'Watch out!' Mitch yelled, but he was too late. In an instant, he completely lost control. As he flipped his front wheel back to rebalance, he clipped the back of Sam's back wheel, and suddenly both of them were hurtling towards the tarmac. The two bikes tangled with each other with a loud clash of metal. All Sam could do was to put out his right arm to break his fall, but he skidded down the road on his side and screamed with the pain of his shoulder burning as his skin was shredded by the road beneath it.

After the clattering and the screaming, there was a sudden silence. Sam lay still for a minute, half on the road but with his head resting in the thick, wet grass of the verge and he looked up to the sky as he tried to work out what part of him hurt the most. His shoulder felt like it was on fire, but his knee was aching too. He tried to move his leg. Not too bad. He raised it and bent it. Still not too bad. And then he heard the groaning. That definitely was bad. That wasn't him. That was Mitch.

Sam looked back up the hill. Mitch was lying there, ten metres away, and he wasn't moving. Sam staggered up to him. Mitch looked bad, like he was tangled in metal. It seemed that he had two bikes wrapped round him. His arm was sticking out at a strange angle and he was moaning through gritted teeth, clearly trying to stop himself from screaming.

'Which bit hurts?' Sam said, standing over him.

'Everything hurts!' Mitch yelled. He couldn't hold back the pain any more. 'Everything hurts so much! My arm! My leg! My right foot! It all hurts!'

Sam gingerly knelt down beside his friend and started to disentangle him. He lifted one bike away. That wasn't too bad. But then he had to slightly lift

Mitch's left arm – the one that was at a funny angle – to free him from the other and Mitch yelled out from the pain. And then he tried to roll Mitch on to his side.

Mitch was a mess. He had bloody marks down his face. His left arm looked weird – horribly weird – and his right leg seemed dead, numb. Mitch could hardly move it.

Sam patted his pockets and took out his mobile phone. He dialled 999 and got no answer. He tried again. Typical! No signal. So he picked up his bike. It was scratched, but it wasn't broken.

'Mitch, I'm going to have to ride ahead. I need to get to a place where I can get a signal and then I'll call for an ambulance, OK?'

Mitch nodded and Sam cycled off. It wasn't easy riding a bike when you've smashed your leg and shredded your shoulder, but he had to help his friend.

Two hours later, they were in hospital. Sam got patched up; it really stung when they wiped his shoulder clean, but he was OK.

Mitch wasn't though. He was in bad shape. The problem with the left arm wasn't actually the arm but the shoulder. He'd dislocated it. That was a bad injury, but not the end of the world. His leg was a different matter though. His knee was smashed, but the real problem was his foot. The impact of the fall had twisted his ankle viciously, ripping the ankle joint and the tendons and ligaments around it. It takes a long time for an injury like that to heal.

It wasn't the end of the world, but it was most definitely the end of Mitch's Olympic dream.

★ 23 ★

THE INQUEST

That crash was nearly the end of Sam's Olympic dream too, but not because of his injuries.

Two days later, he walked into the velodrome and straight into trouble. He'd barely got through the door when he was told that the Professor wanted to see him in his office. And he'd barely got through the door of the Secret Squirrel Club when he realized what the problem was.

The problem was Mac.

'Sit down, Sam,' the Professor said sternly. 'I'll get straight to the point. Mac here believes the accident was your fault. He says you've been a danger on a bike for too long. He thinks you're too young, too much of a risk, too dangerous to ride in the London Olympics. What do you say to that?'

Sam looked at Mac. He was red-faced, angry, as though he'd been shouting. 'I disagree,' Sam said calmly. It felt like he'd been sent to see the headmaster, but he knew he was in the right. At school, situations like this used to make him scared, but he was sure of himself now. 'First, the crash wasn't my fault. I was in front. If I was drafting behind, you could've blamed me, but I wasn't. And second, I'm not a dangerous rider. I'll take risks and I'll push my chances, but that's only because I'm so good at handling a bike. I don't want to sound arrogant, but the only reason it looks as though I'm dangerous is because I know how good I am.'

The Professor looked back at Mac. 'Anything more to add?'

Mac's eyes widened. 'You know my opinion. This boy's a liability. A danger. I think he should be cut from the programme.'

The Professor took a deep breath, as if he was assessing the situation. 'OK,' he said. 'Give me twenty-four hours. I'll make a decision tomorrow.'

Sam was shocked. The crash had not been his fault – he was sure of it. It couldn't have been. He replayed it in his mind over and over again, and he continued to do so until early that evening when he was making his way to Mitch's house. He had to see him. He needed to talk.

Mitch's mother opened the door and showed him into the sitting room. Mitch still looked bad; his arm was in a sling, his leg was in plaster, and the scar marks down his face made him look like he'd been in a really mean fight.

'Nice to see you, mate,' he said. 'Can you believe

that they used to call me the Machine? Well, the Machine is now completely broken.' He chuckled. It was clear he was trying to look on the bright side.

'Good to see you too,' Sam said. He'd been thinking all day about what to say to Mitch and he still hadn't thought of anything. 'I'm so sorry about what happened.'

'Hey,' Mitch said firmly. 'Don't you apologize. It wasn't your fault. It was never your fault. It was me. I might sometimes be faster than you on a bike, but I'm not as skilful. You wouldn't have crashed, but I was too close. My fault. And I've told the Professor that too.'

'Really?'

'Yes. He rang me a couple of hours ago. I told him exactly what happened.'

'Thanks, Mitch.'

'No worries, mate. The only thing you've got to worry about now is winning the Olympics.' He smiled at Sam. 'No pressure there then.'

'I don't think it's quite that simple,' Sam said.

'I hope it is,' Mitch said. 'Look, they need you in the Olympic team, Sam. You're the best there is. Go and get us a medal!'

'What about you though?'

'Don't worry about me. I'm focusing on the next Olympics. We'll go to Rio together. For this one, you're on your own.'

*

The next morning Sam walked into the velodrome feeling more nervous than he ever had done in his life. He hadn't felt this bad when he took his A levels and he'd never felt this nervous before a bike race. He used to think that watching City play Man United stressed him out, but this was on another level altogether.

He didn't say hello to anyone. He just walked straight downstairs to the Secret Squirrel Club. And, sure enough, the Professor was waiting for him. But this time he was on his own. There was no sign of Mac.

'Sit down, Sam,' he said. 'Now, I want you to know this: I think you're a fabulous bike-rider. I don't think you're dangerous, I think you're good. Very good. And I know the crash wasn't your fault. Mitch was pretty clear about that.'

'Good,' said Sam.

'So you'd better get back upstairs and get on with training.'

'OK.' Sam still felt slightly confused. 'So does that mean this issue is over now?'

'It does. Over, dead and buried and forgotten about. And think about it, Sam, you're now first choice to ride in the keirin in the Olympics. How does that make you feel?'

'Er, kind of excited. Kind of good.'

'Excellent.'

Sam got up to go and, just as he was at the door,

the Professor called him back. 'Oh yes, just one other thing.'

'Yes?'

'No need to worry about Mac. I don't think we'll be seeing him again.'

'Really?'

'Afraid so,' he said. 'He lost an argument and he didn't like it so he's walked out. Resigned. So it's up to you now, Sam.'

'What do you mean – it's up to me?'

'What I mean is I believe you're more useful to the British Olympic team than he is. It's up to you now to prove me right.'

★ 24 ★

THE SECRET SQUIRREL DELIVERS

As the weeks slowly passed, the Olympics got closer. And as they got closer, Sam believed more and more that he'd be the rider selected to race the keirin in them. In the Manchester velodrome the coaches sometimes organized practice races and with every victory Sam's self-belief grew. More and more, he felt he knew what he was doing. He grew more confident of how to position himself in a crowded group of riders and which wheel to follow. And if it came to karate on wheels, he knew he could handle that too.

His way of thinking grew too. A few weeks ago, he used to think: *Will I get into Team GB?* But now he was thinking: *If I go, will I get a medal?* And as the Games approached, his life became almost completely dedicated to his bike. The only time he ever saw Grandad was when he arrived unannounced in the velodrome and sat there quietly to watch the training. Sam loved it when he knew that his grandfather was up there in the stands looking down on him.

'I'm so proud of you,' Grandad said to him one day after training, kissing him gently on the forehead. 'I can't believe I once hoped you'd be a footballer. This is much better. Since you found cycling, Sam, you've turned into a real man!'

Sam loved that. But he knew he mustn't be distracted. He knew that he had to pour his every effort into the Olympics. So he wrote down on a piece of paper what the Professor had said to him and he stuck the piece of paper on the wall next to his bed. Every night before he went to sleep and every morning when he woke up, he saw the same message again and again: '*If you work hard enough, you could compete in the Games.*'

Eventually, the day came when he discovered what the Professor had been doing behind the padlocked door. This was exciting. This was the moment he'd been waiting for.

Sam and the other senior riders had just finished a training session when they were told that the Professor wanted to see them in the Secret Squirrel Club. All of them, together. And down there the Professor seemed to turn from a Secret Squirrel into Santa Claus.

'Sit down, everyone, because now's the time to show you what we've been doing down here.' And so the Professor began.

He gave all the riders a new helmet. Sam had never seen a helmet like this before. It had grooves down the side and a kind of tail down the back, a stripe down the top and air vents through the middle. And it was so light. It looked like something from a science-fiction movie. It was beautiful and it had his name inscribed on the inside of the strap. His name.

The Professor then gave all the riders a new bike suit. It was called a skinsuit. The material was stretchy and tight, kind of rubbery and elastic. It had a massive Union Jack across the front. And again, the one given to Sam had his name printed into the back of the neck. His name.

Finally, he gave them all their own pair of gloves. And, yes, Sam's gloves had his name in too. His name.

'What you need to know,' the Professor then explained, 'is this. We're very confident that these helmets are the fastest you'll see in the London Olympic velodrome. We're also confident that your skinsuits will be the fastest, and that even your gloves will be the fastest too.'

Sam put his hand up immediately. He was confused. 'What do you mean? How can our gloves be the fastest?'

'Good question, Sam,' the Professor said. 'It's kind of all to do with physics, science, and it's pretty cool. The fact is that some shapes and some materials travel faster through the air. If you think about it, a ball of wool travels much slower than a golf ball, doesn't it? So what we wanted to find out was what helmet travels the fastest? What's the best shape and the best material? And we've done so much scientific testing on these three pieces of kit, you would not believe it. We even went to a factory where they build Formula one motor-racing cars to test them. This is state-of-the-art stuff – and it's for you and no one else.

'And, if you're all wondering why your names are on the kit, this is the reason: you sixteen riders in this room are going to the Olympics. You've been selected for the team. You'll be the fifteen who'll represent us in London 2012. Congratulations!'

Sam could barely wait. As soon as the meeting was over, he took his phone out of his pocket and started texting. First to his mum, then to Mitch, then to Mr Parrott, his thumbs working fast over the phone keypad:

I've done it! I've got into the team. I'm going to be in the Olympics!

But there was no use texting Grandad. He didn't even have a mobile phone. So Sam rang him at home and could hardly stop the words tumbling out of his mouth. 'I've done it, I've done it, Grandad!' he said. 'I'm going to the Games!'

Down the other end of the line, Grandad went quiet. 'Well done, son!' he said very softly. But Sam could hear why Grandad was so quiet: he was crying. He was crying tears of joy.

★ 25 ★

BEHOLD THE OLYMPICS!

Sam was excited about the Olympics. Of course he was. But there was so much he hadn't thought about:

1. *The media.* The only paper he'd ever been in before was the *Stockport Independent.* But suddenly he was in all the big national newspapers under big fat headlines that all asked the same kind of questions: 'Who is this kid?' 'Anyone heard of mystery boy Sam the cyclist?' and 'Unknown and nineteen, the new Olympic mystery star'.

   That was all quite funny, but it got funnier still. The next day he had to give an interview to six different journalists at the same time and they seemed to really like the story of the newspaper round he did for Mr Parrott. And so the day after that, when he opened the papers, he found his face everywhere again and they all called him 'The paper-round rider' or 'The Olympic newspaper pedaller' or 'The paper-boy Olympian'.

2. *All the kit.* With the other cyclists, he'd been told, 'You're going to Loughborough tomorrow.' And when he'd replied, 'But I'm supposed to be working for Mr Parrott tomorrow,' he got very short shrift: 'No, you're not.'

So he went to Loughborough and brought back so much kit he couldn't believe it. He particularly liked his Team GB toothbrush. He couldn't understand why he got ten pairs of Team GB pants. And what was he supposed to do with a Team GB umbrella? When he got home, he gave the umbrella to Mr Parrott and five pairs of pants to Mitch. Mitch thought that was hilarious.

3. *The tickets.* Suddenly, everyone wanted to go to the Games. His mum wanted tickets, Grandad wanted them, Mitch had only one ticket and that was for the swimming and Mr Parrott wanted tickets for his whole family. Both Adam and Chris from school texted him asking for tickets – and yet he didn't have any for them. All he was told was that he'd be given two tickets for the events he was racing. That was easy – they'd go to Mum and Grandad – but that didn't stop everyone wanting to speak to him, or texting him. But all Sam wanted was to get to the Games.

So at last, when Sam got to London, it felt brilliant. He was here, at the Olympic Games! But there were so many other things he hadn't considered:

4. *The Olympic Village*. This was where he lived; this was where all the Olympians lived. Even Usain Bolt and Michael Phelps – they all lived here! And it was huge; it wasn't a village. Places like Freshton and Twizzlebury and Reakton were villages. The Olympic Village was more like a city!

5. *Being in the team*. In Team GB. Suddenly, he was teammates with famous people like Paula Radcliffe and Rebecca Adlington and Tom Daley. Sam couldn't believe it. They were all a team together and everyone was so incredibly friendly. And you could always spot your GB teammates, Sam found, because every day they'd be told what to wear: your red polo shirt, your blue polo shirt or your white one. It was like a uniform. The GB team were united in trying to win medals for team and country. These were the home Olympics. Everyone, it seemed, was so proud.

6. *The Opening Ceremony*. Well, what he hadn't thought about was the fact that he wasn't allowed to march in it. None of the cyclists were. That was the Professor's rule. He said that the Opening Ceremony involved too much time standing around. And standing around, he added, wasn't likely to help anyone win a medal.

There were two more things though that occupied Sam's mind:

- *Winning.* Everything now was all about winning a medal. As the keirin got closer, that was all Sam could think about. A medal. He wanted one so badly. He wanted to win a medal for his mum and for Grandad. He wanted to win the medal that his great-grandfather never got to win all those years ago.
- *Chen.* Sam thought about how good he was, how clever his tactics were and he wondered how he could possibly beat him.

And then, on his third day in the Olympic Village, Sam finally spotted his Chinese friend. It was in the Olympic Village food hall, which just so happened to be the biggest food hall he'd ever seen. Sam was eating with a big crowd of the GB team – some of the swimmers, some of the triathletes, some hockey players and a couple from the taekwondo team – and they were talking about training and who trained the hardest. How many hours do you train a week? How much does it hurt? How many times have you been sick because the training was so hard? Has it ever hurt so much that you cried?

The swimmers were very insistent that they trained the hardest. The triathletes claimed that they vomited the most. Sam then insisted that nobody felt more physical pain than he did. And the hockey players disagreed with everyone. And they were all laughing.

And then suddenly there he was – across the other side of the room – his friend, his rival, Chen. Sam left the table immediately and walked over slowly, turning over in his mind what he wanted to say and how, in Mandarin, he was going to say it.

'Chen!' he said. '*Ni hao!*' Hello was the easy bit.

Chen turned to him and his eyes brightened. He got up from his chair immediately and wrapped Sam in a warm hug. He seemed happy to see Sam too.

'We will race against each other in the keirin?' Chen asked.

'Yes,' Sam said. 'You will have to give me a chance.'

Chen laughed and then asked, 'Mitch? Where is my other friend Mitch?'

'Injured,' Sam replied. 'But he says I have to win the keirin for him.'

'Ah! I think you will win it, Sam,' Chen said. 'You are the gold-medal man.'

Sam thought that was strange, but he was just so pleased to see Chen. They sat down and started chatting again. They talked about Mitch and his injury. And they talked about Japan and the Olympic keirin competition.

'Watch out for Shane Cooper,' Chen said.

'The Australian?'

'Yes,' Chen said. 'He is good. Very good. And very physical. He likes to turn it into a fight.'

'Well, we have plenty of experience of that,' Sam said.

They were quiet for a minute and then Sam finally put to his friend the questions he really wanted to ask: 'Are you OK, Chen? Where is that man in the tracksuit who was with you in Japan?'

'He is not in here now,' Chen said, 'so I can talk to you. But sometimes he is and then I cannot. I am still not happy, Sam. Tell me, do you love cycling? Do you love your sport?'

'Yes,' Sam answered. 'Of course I do.'

'That is what I want, Sam,' Chen said. 'I want to love my cycling again.' He paused for thought and then carried on. 'Is Mitch coming to see the Olympic Games?'

'Yes,' Sam chuckled. 'But he could only get tickets for the swimming tomorrow.'

'He is coming tomorrow?'

'Yes.'

'Good,' Chen said. Then he paused, smiled at Sam and said, very slowly, in perfect English: 'I like your beautiful country!'

Sam nearly fell off his chair. 'Chen! You speak English!'

Chen smiled and spoke the same slow English again. 'Very badly I speak English,' he said. 'I have been practising hard.'

'Very good!' said Sam. 'Now I say goodbye. I will see you next Tuesday. Then we will race for gold!'

★ 26 ★

HOT IN THE HEATS

The Olympic keirin competition was held over a whole day. There were three rounds: the first was on Tuesday morning, and the second and final were later in the afternoon. There were six riders in each heat and the first two would go through from each round.

When Tuesday morning arrived, Sam felt so ready that he couldn't wait to get to the velodrome. He felt he'd been waiting for this moment all his life. He chuckled to himself as he walked in; he'd heard all about this place with its huge wavy roof. Because of the roof, it had been nicknamed the Giant Pringle. Sam just hoped that the Pringle would bring him luck.

The atmosphere in the velodrome was awesome. The place was packed. There were 6,000 seats in there and all of them were full, and it seemed that pretty much every one of those 6,000 people was cheering for Team GB. Sam took a moment to look around and listen. It was so loud. He pinched himself. He couldn't believe it. This was it. This was the moment he'd been waiting for. It was time to do the business.

He looked around for his mum and Grandad. He couldn't see them, but that was probably a good thing. He knew how emotional Grandad would get and he didn't want him to cry again. He thought to himself, *The only time I want Grandad to cry is when I've got a medal hanging round my neck.*

In the centre of the velodrome were the paddocks. This was where all the teams were based, where the coaches were and the mechanics, and where the riders would warm up for their races. The GB paddock was in the corner, nice and big, next to Spain and New Zealand. But it was Australia that Sam was concerned about. Australia and that man Chen had warned him about, Shane Cooper.

He could see Chen, a few metres away from the GB paddock, preparing with the China team. He tried to catch his eye, but Chen was concentrating hard, talking to the man in the tracksuit. Sam knew for sure that, though they were normally friends, now they were rivals.

But he also knew he had one big advantage: the equipment from the Secret Squirrel Club. And there was something else that he hoped might work in his favour: he was the new boy around here. Apart from Chen, no one in the other teams had really heard of him, and they certainly hadn't raced him before. So he might be able to take them by surprise.

As Sam started to warm up, he chatted to the Professor, trying to remain relaxed. The Professor was good like that; he knew the one easy way to distract Sam, to get him to stay calm, was to talk about Manchester City.

'So who do you think City will buy for next season?' he asked. 'Do you think City will ever run out of money?' And they chatted away, about the Premiership, and whether the Manchester clubs would do better in Europe next season, and whether anyone would ever be as good as the Spanish clubs again. And then suddenly the Professor said, 'Right, Sam, ten minutes till your heat.'

Sam got his bike ready, and his gloves and his helmet. He felt good. He didn't feel happy about the fact that he had Shane Cooper in his heat, but he was confident and he knew his tactics: stick on Shane's wheel and you'll be fine.

On the track, Sam and the other riders waited. There was a nervous silence among them. They put their helmets and gloves on. They were all there except for Cooper. And then finally, as Cooper approached them, Sam saw something that he could not believe. Cooper's helmet.

It wasn't possible. Surely it wasn't possible. It had grooves down the side and a kind of tail down the back, a stripe down the top and air vents through the middle. It looked like something from a science-fiction movie. In fact, it looked exactly like Sam's helmet. It looked the same as every helmet worn by every rider in the whole British team.

How could he have got it? Could he have had access to the Secret Squirrel Club? Sam felt completely deflated. He felt as though someone had just punched him in the stomach. But he had to pull himself together. He had to race.

However, Cooper didn't help: he pulled his helmet on and turned immediately to Sam. 'Hey, nice headgear, boy!' he said. And he chuckled. It was as if he was laughing at Sam and the GB team. And strangely it was as if he knew who Sam was too.

'Come on,' Sam said to himself. 'If he's going to make you angry, you'll just have to beat him in the final.'

By the time the race started, Sam was more determined than ever. As soon as they started, he followed Cooper close, really close – he wasn't going to let him go anywhere. He stuck to him like glue. In fact, he stuck to him so hard that Cooper kept on looking back over his shoulder; he didn't like it. Sam felt good. He waited, waited, waited on Cooper's wheel for the moment to make his move.

And then Cooper pulled a stunt that Sam had never seen in his life. He suddenly slowed down – in fact, he slowed so much that Sam went right into the back of him and lost his balance; he started tipping over to the left and thought he was going to fall. For the flash of a microsecond, he thought his Olympics were over. He hauled his weight back over to the other side and steadied the bike. He was OK, but the damage had already been done. Sam had slipped to the back of the group, and Cooper was way out ahead in front.

Sam had one lap to catch up. He hammered down on his pedals, harder and more furiously than ever before in his life. He wasn't going to let go easily. He started catching the others. He went past one, then two more. He was never going to catch Cooper, but that didn't matter. All that mattered was that he finished second.

He had one more rider to catch. One more bend and then the finish. Sam could hear the screaming and cheering of the crowd as he gave chase. He was almost alongside him. '*Come on! Come on!*'

He realized that the person shouting 'Come on!' was himself.

He powered forward and strained for the line. He'd done it. Cooper had nearly killed him off, but he was still alive. He sat up in the saddle and let the momentum from the bike take him round the track as he slowly lost speed. He felt relief. He felt happy.

And then Sam spotted something else. Suddenly, everything made sense. Cooper, the helmet, everything. Because there in the crowd, sitting with two other coaches, was Mac. And the coaches he was sitting with both had yellow and green Australia tracksuits on. And Mac's was the same. He'd changed sides and had taken the secrets of the Secret Squirrel Club with him.

When Sam got back to the Team GB paddock, he could hardly talk quickly enough. He was so furious.

'Did you see? Did you see? The helmet!' he said to the Professor. 'It's Mac! It's him! It was Mac!'

The Professor stayed completely calm. He said nothing while Sam blurted out everything he had to say. And then, when he finally stopped, gasping for breath, the Professor said, 'Look, Sam, we know. We all know. We saw Mac too. He's copied our design. It's wrong. It's foul play. But there's nothing we can do. There's only one way to get our revenge, and that's by you beating Cooper in the final.'

No matter how calm the Professor might be, Sam still wanted to go straight over to the Australian paddock and tell Cooper what he thought of him. He also wanted to go and confront Mac in his seat – and he didn't know what he'd do to him if he found him! But he also knew that the Professor was right. There was only one thing to do: if he wanted to get revenge on Mac, he had to beat Cooper.

First, he had to qualify through his second-round race and that wasn't so hard. He was in a race with

Chen, and Chen beat him easily. No surprise there. Chen was as brilliant as he had been the year previously in Japan. But Sam stuck as close as he could to Chen's wheel and came through in second place. So he was in the final. He had a chance to get a medal. All he had to do was grab it.

★ 27 ★

OLYMPIC FINAL

This was the moment Sam had been dreaming of ever since Grandad first told him about his great-grandfather and his courage on a bicycle in the Second World War. It was strange, Sam thought, to think that his great-grandfather, a man he'd never met, was one of the reasons he wanted to win so much.

He looked at his phone. There were so many texts from people wishing him good luck that he didn't even have time to read them all. He scrolled down and read the one from Mitch:

> Stick to Chen's wheel. You're the most skilful bike-rider I've ever known. So stick with Chen and you'll get yourself a medal.

Good advice. He scrolled down a bit further and read the text from Mr Parrott.

> I am so proud of you. But when you've finished at the Olympics will you please come back and do the newspaper round again!

That made Sam laugh. Sam then went on Twitter and posted a short message to his followers:

This is the biggest day of my life!

The final was going to be a great race. Sam knew perfectly well how good Chen was and he'd already had one experience of how dangerous Shane Cooper was. Plus, Cooper had the advantage of the same bike helmet. That certainly didn't help. But Sam was also concerned about a rider from New Zealand whom everyone was talking about – Ben Roberts – who was very fast.

There were two riders whom Sam was confident he could beat, one from Japan and an American. Though Sam thought he was better than them, he also knew that in a keirin anything can happen. However, he knew what he had to do and he knew Mitch was right. He had to stick to Chen.

Down at the Pringle, Sam prepared for his race in the usual way. He made sure his bike was ready; he made sure he had his equipment, his helmet and his gloves, and then he started warming up.

As usual, the Professor started talking to him about football and now he had a great topic. 'What is your all-time greatest-ever Man City side? If you had to pick the best eleven from any era, who'd be in your team? How many of the current squad make it? And would Mario Balotelli get in or is he just too mad?'

Sam loved that. He loved talking about all the great old players that Grandad always used to go on and on about. Sam hadn't seen them play, but he felt he knew them as if they were part of the family. One by one, they went through every position in the team, and they'd just got into a debate about the qualities of David Silva when the Professor said, 'Right, enough of that. We've got an Olympic medal to win. You're on in twenty minutes.'

Sam was astonished. The time had flown by. He was about to race for gold.

He started gathering his equipment together and looked across the paddocks. The Australians all seemed calm. Mac was now in the paddock and was talking to Cooper with a serious look on his face. Cooper was listening hard. It looked as though they were talking tactics.

Over in the New Zealand paddock, Ben Roberts was strapping on his helmet. Sam thought he looked nervous. And there was something of a commotion in the Chinese paddock. That was unusual. The Chinese were always so calm.

Sam started wheeling his bike over to the track. The American was already there. They were joined by Roberts, who was taking fast deep breaths, as if he was scared, and then the Japanese rider and then Cooper.

Cooper glared at Sam, walked up to him and said

under his breath, 'You sit on my wheel again, mate, and your Olympics are over!'

But Sam was quick with his response. He wasn't scared of people talking like that. 'Why would I sit on your wheel, Cooper? You're not going to be going fast enough!' And, before Cooper could respond, he moved away. Sam didn't want to talk, he didn't want to trade insults with the Australian. He felt nervous and he just wanted to race.

Everyone was waiting for Chen, but there was still something of a commotion in the Chinese paddock. Sam couldn't see him anywhere. Where was he? The coaches in the Chinese camp started shouting at each other. Sam saw the familiar sight of Chen's coach; two other coaches were shouting at him angrily.

The stadium announcer then made a loud announcement: 'Could Chen Kwailam please come to the track.' A minute later, the announcement was repeated: 'Could Chen Kwailam please come to the track.' But there was no sign of him. This was the Olympic final and he'd gone missing.

Sam and the other riders started getting fidgety. Cooper shouted at one of the officials, 'Come on! If he's not here, we'll have to race without him.'

'No!' Sam said firmly. 'We should wait for him. He's qualified for the final so he should be allowed to race in it.'

But still Chen didn't appear.

The official came over and explained the situation to Sam and the other four riders. 'We don't know where he is, I'm afraid,' he said. 'We've told the Chinese team: we can delay the final by another five minutes, but, if he's not here by then, you five will race the Olympic final without him.'

The Chinese coaches were now arguing with each other and shrugging their shoulders. They seemed to have no idea where he was. Cooper looked happy; he knew that in a few minutes' time, with no Chen in the race, his chances of getting the gold medal could improve massively.

And Sam had to think hard and quick. If Chen didn't show up, then what would he do? He'd have to change his tactics. Whose wheel would he draft behind? He was still thinking about that when there was another announcement in the stadium: 'The men's keirin Olympic final will start in two minutes. There will be just five riders. Chen Kwailam has been defaulted from the race.'

Defaulted? Sam was shocked. There were now five riders fighting for three medals. Cooper looked delighted.

The race set off and the riders followed the derny round and round the track. Roberts was looking around him; he still seemed nervous. The American was right behind the derny. The Japanese rider was at the back. And then Sam suddenly had an idea, a new plan, and pulled slightly to the side; he'd decided exactly what he was going to do. It was a dangerous tactic, but he liked it.

The second the derny pulled over, Sam sped back into the pack of riders and locked on to Cooper's back wheel. It was exactly what Cooper had told him not to do. He stuck to it closely, even closer than the last time. He watched carefully and he waited. He wouldn't let Cooper go. And he knew that Cooper knew exactly where he was. He turned his head very slightly to check. This is exactly what Sam had expected. Cooper looked agitated, but Sam wouldn't budge.

And then suddenly Cooper did it again. Just as he had in their heat, he abruptly slowed down. But this time Sam was ready. He knew it was coming. And the very moment that Cooper slowed, Sam swung out. Again, their bikes touched, but Sam was ready and he leaned into Cooper and darted past him. This time it was Cooper who lost balance. His bike wobbled first to the right, and then to the left where it hit the Japanese rider. There was a huge smash as Cooper and the Japanese rider both screamed and came clattering to the ground. Their race was over. Cooper was out.

But Sam had no time to look round and enjoy the sight. All he could think about was the line. The gold medal.

He was alongside Roberts who was looking confident and strong. Stronger than he had all day.

The American was behind them. It was a straight race, Sam versus Roberts for gold.

They came off the final bend side by side. The volume of the crowd went up and up, but Sam could hear nothing; all he could concentrate on was the line and the pumping, pumping of his legs. He felt the pain in his muscles, but he fought it as he had done all his life. He could beat the pain. He felt like he was in slow motion; he felt like he was flying. He rammed the pedals down and edged ahead . . . Centimetres. Was it less than centimetres? Sam and Roberts thundered over the line side by side. But Sam was ahead. He knew he was ahead.

He knew he was the new Olympic champion.

★ 28 ★

OLYMPIC HERO

Sam could not believe it. He could not believe what was happening.

After going through the line and winning the race, he stood up in his pedals, punched the air and screamed. He didn't know what he screamed. It wasn't really a word. You couldn't spell it. It was just a noise, a very loud noise, with lots of vowels and no consonants.

When you go through the line as fast as he did, it takes a while to slow down, and so he carried on rolling round the track, his arm held aloft in victory. And as he went round, everyone in the Giant Pringle stood up and cheered him. The noise was amazing. They were cheering for him! For the new Olympic champion!

As he rode past, one fan stretched out her arm to give him a Union Jack flag and he grabbed it and then cycled on round with the Union Jack held out behind him.

Ben Roberts was still on the track too, lapping up

the applause as well. He looked delighted to have won the silver. Sam slowed down and as they cycled round together, Sam shook Ben's hand. 'Well done, Ben. That was some finish!' he said.

'I can't believe that stunt you pulled on Cooper!' Ben replied. 'That was a pretty cool piece of bike-riding, Sam.'

In the paddock below, they could see Cooper. And they could see Mac. Both of them looked stunned. Neither of them was talking.

'Do you know what happened to Chen?' Sam asked.

'No idea, mate!' Ben replied. 'But it kind of suited me that he never made it.'

'You're right,' Sam said. 'If Chen had been here, there's no way I'd be Olympic champion.'

'Hey, let it go, Sam!' Ben said. 'Chen didn't make it to the startline. You're the Olympic champion. You deserve it. Enjoy!'

Ben was right. And, just as Ben said it, Sam caught a glimpse of his mum and Grandad. They had left their seats and run down the steps to the side of the track. Sam pulled over immediately, stopped right by them, leaned over the side of the track and almost collapsed into their arms. He felt his mum's face against his and it was wet with tears. And Grandad was grabbing him and planting a huge, wet kiss on his forehead.

'You did it, son!' he screamed. Sure enough, he

was crying too. And he was shouting at the top of his voice: 'You did it, son! You said you'd do it and you did! You did it, son! You did it!'

Sam leaned back a bit to look at them both. The tears were still rolling down his mum's face. 'Why're you crying, Mum?' Sam had to shout to make himself heard above all the cheering around him.

'I'm so proud, Sam!' she said, and still she couldn't stop herself crying. 'I'm just so, so proud!'

★ 29 ★

THE END

When you're the new Olympic champion, it sometimes seems that the celebrations never end. That, at least, is how it felt for Sam.

He loved being Olympic champ. He loved getting his medal, he loved standing on top of the rostrum and singing the national anthem. And as he stood there singing, he thought about all the people who'd helped get him to the top of the world: his mum, Grandad, Mr Parrott, the Professor, Mitch. He even thought about Nate and everyone at school. What would they be thinking now?

Later that evening, when he walked back into the Olympic Village, he still wore his gold medal around his neck and different sportsmen and women from all over the world stopped and congratulated him in languages that he'd never heard before. In fact, it seemed that the congratulating would never cease. The media certainly kept going with it. The next day they went on and on about how 'two years ago this kid was doing a newspaper round on a bike and now he's winning the Olympics on one'. They also liked the fact that Sam was so young. The *Daily Express* seemed to find it very funny and said, 'This boy hasn't yet learned how to drive a car, yet he can handle a bicycle better than anyone else in the world.'

It wasn't until the day after the race that Sam sat down with some more journalists and told them the story that he really wanted to tell. He told them about his great-grandfather, and how he'd been a cyclist and would have gone to the Helsinki Olympic Games in 1940, and had ended up getting shot on his bike in the Second World War instead. The journalists seemed to like that story too.

In fact, Sam thought, the media seemed fascinated by everything about him and his Olympic victory apart from one part of it which had been completely forgotten about. No one knew where Chen was and no one seemed particularly interested either. However, Sam never stopped looking out for him. Every time he went into the food hall in the Olympic Village, he'd cast an eye around every table in the room. But he never got a glimpse of him. He soon started also looking out for the coach – the one in the tracksuit top – but he never saw him either. It was so incredibly weird.

And then the days passed and the end of the Games was upon him. Sam wondered seriously if he'd ever see Chen again, or even find out what had happened to him.

*

Eventually, Sam had to stop thinking about Chen. The Olympics had been the most amazing time in the whole of his life, but they were soon over. And though Sam was sad to say goodbye to London, he had one last celebration to look forward to: his homecoming party. And there was only one place where they could possibly hold it – the very place where his whole story had started: Anything & Everything.

It was a funny place for a party – a shop that sold newspapers and baked beans and was now starting to sell bicycles too – but still it felt right. Mr Parrott had set it up brilliantly. He'd moved the baked beans and the shelves of bread and milk to the side and had hung Sam's Giant bike from the ceiling as if it was some kind of special guest. And he'd also invited everyone Sam wanted to the party.

Even Nate pitched up which surprised Sam, but Mr Parrott explained how helpful he'd become. Ever since Sam had stopped working at the shop, Nate had filled in for him. Sam remembered all too well that day all those years ago when Mr Parrott had been so furious with Nate. The fact that he was now prepared to give him work again showed that Nate had learned from his mistakes.

Sam talked to everyone at the party and he showed them all his medal. And Grandad, who was still so proud, made sure he told everyone how Sam had won the race – forgetting that they'd all probably watched it on TV over and over again.

After a while, there was a late arrival. It was Mitch. Sam had wondered where he'd got to and he was about to give his old friend a massive hug when Mitch said, 'Hang on, mate, hang on. Before I start telling you how brilliant you are, there's something I want to say to everyone.'

So Mitch stood in the middle of Anything & Everything and said at the top of his voice, 'Excuse me, everyone. I'd just like to say a few words.' The crowd went quiet and gathered round to hear what he had to say. 'I want to say two things, the first of which is very obvious. Congratulations to my friend Sam. Like everyone here, I'm so proud and so happy for him.'

Sam beamed a huge smile and Mitch carried on. 'The second thing I want to say is this. It's an introduction really. An introduction to a very special friend of mine and Sam's who was very, very keen to be here to celebrate with Sam today. He also happens to be a brilliant cyclist.' Mitch then walked over to the door of the shop. He opened it wide and in walked Chen.

Chen! It really was him! He looked embarrassed, slightly shy, but he had a familiar smile on his face. Sam went straight over and hugged him.

'Chen!' he exclaimed. 'I don't understand! Why? What happened?'

Chen laughed, and in his slow English he said, 'It's a very long story!'

So Sam and Mitch and Chen went into the corner of the shop and sat down, and Mitch and Chen told the story together. As he told it, Chen switched languages, from faltering English to Mandarin and back again. He explained that, when he got to London, he'd emailed Mitch and told him how unhappy he was. He explained how Mitch had come to see him at the Olympic Village one day – the day that Mitch had tickets for the swimming. And how they'd come up with a plan.

'Mitch helped me,' Chen said in English. 'Mitch saved me.'

Mitch then took over telling the story. Chen, he said, had decided that he wanted to leave China; he wanted to win the Olympics, but said he was more interested in leaving his country. He wanted to defect. And Chen had told him that the only time that he'd be able to get away from the man in the tracksuit would be right before the final. The tracksuit-man had said he'd leave him on his own for a break after the second race.

'So it was quite simple,' Mitch said. 'I went to meet Chen in between the second race and the final. He left with me and has been staying with me and my parents in Buxton ever since.'

'I like Buxton,' Chen said and all three of them laughed.

'You should see Chen riding up the Winnats Pass,' Mitch said. 'He's absolutely awesome.'

'But what's he going to do in England?' Sam asked.

'He's going to try and become a professional bike-rider,' Mitch said. 'And, until then, Mr Parrott has already offered him a job as his new newspaper boy.'

Sam laughed. And Mitch and Chen did too. This felt good.

'But, Chen,' Sam said, and he fiddled around in his pocket. 'What about this?' He pulled out his gold medal. 'This should be yours. You should have it. You'd have won that race.'

Chen shook his head. 'Sam, you are Olympic champion. Your medal. You deserve it.'

Sam put the medal away again. 'OK then,' he said. 'But we three need to meet for a training ride tomorrow. We need to start training for the next Olympics. Next time round, we're all going to win a medal!'

CYCLING FINAL STATISTICS

KEIRIN OLYMPIC CHAMPIONS

2000

The keirin was not an Olympic event until the Sydney Games in 2000. The first Olympic keirin was won by Frenchman Florian Rousseau, who was popular because of the strange facial expressions he would pull on the startline which made it look as if his eyes were about to pop out.

2004

The second Olympic keirin was won by Ryan Bayley of Australia. One of Bayley's biggest-ever rivals was a fellow Australian, Shane Perkins. Bayley and Perkins were not friends at all. It didn't help when Perkins then became engaged to Bayley's sister.

2008

The keirin was one of the three gold medals won in Beijing by Chris Hoy, the Scot. The keirin and the sprint are the two events that sprinters can compete in individually in the Olympics (Hoy's other gold was the team sprint).

Hoy, Bayley and Rousseau all won the keirin/sprint double.

BEST-EVER KEIRIN RIDER
Koichi Nakano, a Japanese rider, won the keirin in the world track cycling championships ten years in a row, from 1977 to 1986. It is unlikely that this achievement will ever be matched. It is just unfortunate that there was no keirin in the Olympics when Nakano was at his best because he would almost certainly have won that too.

★ ★ ★ ★ ★ ★ ★ ★ ★ ★ ★ ★ ★ ★ ★ ★ ★

CYCLING RECORDS

82.819 mph   This is the world record speed for a bike on the flat, set by the Canadian cyclist Sam Whittingham. He was set up to break the record, in 2009, on a special bike and at altitude in Nevada, USA.

167.044 mph This is the world record speed reached using drafting. The record was set in 1995 by a Dutch cyclist, Fred Rompelberg, on the Bonneville Salt Flats in Utah, USA. He was riding in the slipstream of a motor dragster.

138 mph This is the fastest-ever speed a bike has reached racing downhill. Downhill racers hit their fastest speeds on snow. This record was set by Eric Barone, a Frenchman known as the Red Baron, in Les Arcs, a ski resort in France, in April 2000. Away from the snow, the record downhill bike speed is also held by Barone: he went to a volcano in Nicaragua in May 2002 and set the record at 107 mph.

56.375 km The most famous record in cycling is the Hour record for the furthest distance cycled in one hour. The record is held by Chris Boardman, who appears in this book. Boardman set the record in 1993. It was then broken again by Scotsman Graeme Obree before Boardman took it again in 1996. After Boardman's last record, the governing body of world cycling – the UCI – constructed rules that declared if you rode a specially constructed bike, like Boardman's, then it was against the rules. Because other riders then returned to standard bikes, Boardman's remains the furthest distance ever completed in an hour.

★ ★ ★ ★ ★ ★ ★ ★ ★ ★ ★ ★ ★ ★ ★

SOME OF GREAT BRITAIN'S FAMOUS OLYMPIC MEDALLISTS

These medallists show how much Olympic cycling has changed over the years.

FREDERICK KEEPING

He competed in the first Olympic Games of the modern era, in Athens in 1896. His event was the twelve-hour race, which was thoroughly tedious as it involved going round and round an outdoor velodrome. Six riders started the race and it was so gruelling that four dropped out and, when the other two finished, their legs were swollen and they were both weeping from the pain. Keeping finished one lap behind the winner, Adolf Schmal of Austria. The twelve-hour race was never held in an Olympics again.

JOHN MATTHEWS AND ARTHUR RUSHEN

They won gold in the 2,000m tandem race in the Athens Games of 1906. Tandem racing – two on the same bike – remained in the Olympic programme until 1972.

TEAM PURSUIT TEAM, 1956

The team pursuit is one of the most fascinating events in the whole Olympics. Four riders have to be technically brilliant, riding close to each other's wheel as they execute a 4km race. The team pursuit has long been a British strength: GB won it first in 1908 and then again 100 years later in Beijing. The bronze medal team of 1956 is notable because one of the quartet was Tommy Simpson, one of the most famous and successful British cyclists of all time, who died on a stage of the Tour de France in 1967.

CHRIS BOARDMAN

After 1920, GB went on a gold medal drought in Olympic cycling; the country still won plenty of medals but just could not get a gold. After 1920, nineteen medals – all silvers and bronzes – were won until 1992 when Boardman shocked the world with his space-age bike, designed by Lotus, which won him the individual pursuit so commandingly that no one else could get close to him.

YVONNE McGREGOR

It was only ninety-two years into the modern Olympics that women's races were finally introduced. Women's racing began in 1988. Twelve years later, in Sydney, in the 3,000m individual pursuit event, Yvonne McGregor, a tough Yorkshire woman, won bronze, the first cycling medal won by a British woman.

CHRIS HOY

Six days before his competition, in Athens in 2004, Hoy cycled over some molten tar in the Olympic village and fell, landing heavily. Luckily his crash took place just in front of the athletes' medical centre. Six days later, he was on the line in a brilliant contest – the 1km time trial, in which athletes take turns to be timed over a kilometre. As Hoy waited, four riders in front of him each broke the Olympic record and Hoy's task looked harder and harder. But Hoy then did exactly the same: he broke the record again and won gold. He did even better in Beijing four years later where he won three gold medals.

THE SUPER-TEAM AT BEIJING

British cyclists ruled the world at the Beijing velodrome. Seven gold medals put them far ahead of any other nation in the world. Sometimes it seemed the other nations were riding for second place. Chris Hoy took three golds, Bradley Wiggins took two, and two British girls, Rebecca Romero and Victoria Pendleton, took gold too. It is unlikely that any national team of any country will ever be this successful again.

NICOLE COOKE

While the riders ruled inside the Beijing velodrome, Cooke was already the queen of the road. The Beijing road race was played out in a heavy downpour but Cooke, a tough girl from Swansea, came off the last bend and into a slow hill to win the final sprint. The Olympic road race gold was the first cycling gold ever won by a British woman and it confirmed her as one of the greatest female road cyclists of all time.

READ ON FOR A SNEAK PEEK

★ ★ ★ ★ ★ ★ ★ ★ ★ ★ ★ ★ ★ ★ ★

RUNNING
FOR GOLD

Can Danny achieve his olympic dream?

★ ★ ★ ★ ★ ★ ★ ★ ★ ★ ★ ★ ★ ★

★ 1 ★

DANNY POWELL

Until 20 May, no one had taken Danny Powell very seriously. They liked him and they kind of guessed that he was extra special because they all knew he could run so blisteringly fast. Wow, could he run fast! Everyone knew he had the quickest pair of feet in the school. In fact, they all knew that Danny could run faster than anyone in any school in the whole of the United Kingdom.

Every summer it seemed, Danny would go to the UK School Games and come back champion. Whenever those UK School Games came round, the following Monday morning you almost knew that your school email inbox at Newham Secondary would deliver the same news: that Danny Powell had won the 100 metres. Again. This meant that he was the best young sprinter in the country. Still. Indeed, pretty much everyone who had ever met Danny knew that, one day, he would be a professional athlete.

But where the whole Danny story got a bit ridiculous

was when he told them that in the summer holidays after his A levels, he was going to beat Usain Bolt.

Oh, yeah, Danny? No one beats Usain Bolt. Usain Bolt is the fastest human being of all time. Dream on, Danny.

Danny hated the idea of being a show-off and so he had not intended to let it slip. He loved to run and he loved to win. It was, by far, the best thing in his life. But he never bragged. Not around school. Nowhere. He never wanted other people to think that he was a show-off, a swank. And so his dream of beating Bolt was one that he kept completely to himself. And if it wasn't for a robbery, from right under his nose, then it would have remained there.

It happened one day during school lunchtime. He wished it hadn't. And it was the stupid thief's fault. Such a stupid, dozy, hopeless thief. Danny was hanging around the school gates, the place he and his mate, loudmouth Anthuan, and a bunch of their mates in the sixth form always hung out at lunchtime.

No one saw the thief coming. He was probably only twenty years old, average in height and average in looks. He wore dark jeans and a dark T-shirt, but they only realized all that afterwards. At the time, all anyone realized was that with one slightly nervous and aggressive sweep of his arm, he had ripped off the shoulder bag that Jess had hanging loosely from her shoulder. He did it with such force that Jess, yelping in shock more than pain, fell to the ground.

Danny knew that it was wrong to get involved. *Keep your nose out of trouble.* That's what his father always told him. So he stood and, for about two seconds, he watched as the bloke hotfooted it down the pavement. A series of thoughts flashed through Danny's mind: *Should I let him go? Should I stay out of trouble? Might I get hurt? And should I stay here and look after Jess?* And then, in that very split second that he had persuaded himself to be cautious and avoid trouble, the thief stopped running and turned, and it seemed that he was smiling. He may just have been panting, out of breath, but from where Danny was standing it seemed that he had a triumphant grin on his face. And that was that. Danny was off.

The sight of Danny Powell at full speed is astonishing. He has a long stride and a natural balance, which combine into a beautiful elegance. So, when he is sprinting, it doesn't look as though he is trying hard – it hardly seems as though his feet touch the ground; it is more as if he is gliding. But, boy, does he move fast.

He flashed like lightning down the road. It was about two seconds before the thief turned again and realized that he was being pursued and, at that stage, his smile disappeared for good. Danny started closing on him quick and as the distance between them was rapidly disappearing, passers-by moved out of the way and stopped and stared. As Danny got even nearer, the difference between his speed and the thief's was so great, it was almost funny. The thief's arms were pumping hard, flailing desperately from side to side but, compared to Danny, he was going so slowly it was like he was running in treacle.

Danny got closer and closer: thirty metres away, twenty-five metres, twenty . . . Suddenly, he was almost able to touch him when the thief turned round, saw that he was beaten and dropped the bag.

And that was when Danny stopped running. He didn't want to catch the thief. What would he have done to him? Fought him? He had never fought anyone; he wouldn't know what to do.

So he just stopped running and picked up Jess's bag. And that was that. End of episode. At least so he thought.

The next day at Newham Secondary, they had school assembly. School assembly was held every Thursday and it was usually pretty dull. During school assembly, Danny and Anthuan and most of their friends would have their mobile phones out and would be busy texting each other. If you got caught with your mobile phone during assembly, it would be confiscated for the rest of the day. But hardly anyone ever got caught, at least not Danny or Anthuan; they were far too smart for that.

Up on the school stage stood the headmaster, Mr McCaffrey. As teachers go, Mr McCaffrey was OK. But he loved the sound of his own voice – and so he loved Thursdays and school assembly because that was his chance to be centre stage and do lots of talking. Mr McCaffrey also had a greying goatee beard that he seemed rather fond of even if he was slightly too old for it. He would stand and talk and stroke his goatee at the same time. Danny often wondered if Mr McCaffrey had any idea that barely anyone ever listened to a word he said.

Danny scrolled down the inbox of his phone. He was hoping for a text from Ricky, his brother. He adored Ricky, but Ricky was a student, away at university, and he never got in touch. Danny hated that. He missed Ricky. But he thought he might get a text from him today.

It was then, suddenly, that Danny's attention to his phone was ripped away. Anthuan gave him a hefty nudge in the ribs with his elbow. 'Dan,' he whispered, out of the side of his mouth. 'Listen up, Dan, he's talking about you.'

Anthuan was right. Up on stage, Mr McCaffrey was babbling on, as ever, but he was now babbling on about a robbery incident the previous day. *Oh no, please no!* thought Danny. He hated the idea of being the centre of attention.

'. . . and this thief thought he had got away with it,' was what Mr McCaffrey was saying, 'but he hadn't accounted for the fact that at Newham Secondary, we happen to have the fastest young schoolboy in the country. So well done, Danny Powell.'

Mr McCaffrey then started clapping and there was a flutter of applause around the school hall. Danny looked down, trying to avoid everyone's stares. But then Mr McCaffrey carried on: 'And so I would like to ask Danny Powell to come up here for a minute.'

Oh no! You can't be serious! thought Danny. But the headmaster was. And it was on stage that the day really took a turn for the worse.

'Danny,' Mr McCaffrey said, turning to him, 'well done. You have made us all proud.'

'Thank you, sir,' Danny replied.

'And here we are, at the start of the athletics season. Have you got any big plans?'

Danny felt flustered. *What should I say?* he thought. So he decided he may as well be honest – and he just said: 'Yes.'

'Would you fancy running in the Olympics?' Mr McCaffrey asked.

'Of course,' Danny replied. 'Who wouldn't?'

'Exactly,' said Mr McCaffrey. 'Good luck, Danny.' And Danny had just started walking off the stage when Mr McCaffrey said: 'One other thing, Danny . . .' So Danny stopped. '. . . I don't suppose you could beat Usain Bolt, could you?'

Danny paused. *What should I say? What should I say?* And before he could stop himself, he told the truth. 'It's going to be tough, but that's certainly the plan, sir.'

The second that Danny had let that sentence fly from his mouth, he wanted to catch it and take it back again. The school hall erupted with squeals and whistles and quite a lot of laughter. And Danny couldn't stand people laughing at him.

Five minutes later, when assembly was over, the school hall had emptied and the students had piled out into the open air, he was made to feel even worse. 'Dream on, Danny!' was the first comment that was flung his way. 'Danny, I hear Usain Bolt's really scared.' 'Danny, Bolt could beat you on one leg.' And: 'Danny, what planet are you on? Come back down to earth, you might enjoy it down here.'

Ha! Ha! Very funny, the lot of you, thought Danny as he turned left out of the school hall towards the classrooms. He hated people thinking he was arrogant. But what he hated the most was the idea that people didn't believe in him, that they should laugh at the very idea that he was going to beat Usain Bolt. *I'll prove them all wrong*, he said to himself. 'Bolt could beat you on one leg,' they said. How he wanted to ram those comments down their precious little throats.

For the rest of the day, Danny was not allowed to forget it. Most people were too scared to say anything, but he could see them smirking to each other.

Some were brave enough to comment. 'Usain's got no chance!' was one sarcastic comment. He hated that.

'Good luck against Bolt!' were the words of one younger boy. And he probably meant it, but Danny didn't like that either.

At the end of the school day, feeling thoroughly dispirited, Dan sought out the company of Anthuan. But that didn't turn out to be a very good idea either.

'Are you coming out to the movies tomorrow night, Dan?' he asked.

'I can't,' Danny replied. 'I've got to train, haven't I?'

'We're *all* going,' Anthuan said, slightly pleadingly, as if trying to play on Danny's conscience.

'I just can't,' Danny replied, shrugging. 'You know that. Training. I've got to train. I've *always* got to train.'

Anthuan seemed disappointed and went quiet. They walked out of the school gates together. And then Anthuan asked him a question that really surprised him. And the way he asked it suggested that he was slightly uncomfortable about it himself.

'Dan,' he said, 'do you really think you could beat Usain Bolt?'

Danny stopped walking, paused for a second and then answered: 'Ant, I know it sounds crazy, and I know I sound stupid when I say it. But this is my dream. The Olympics are coming. I've got a one in a million chance of beating that guy. So yes, I do think I have a chance. It's a slim one, but it's still a chance. What do you think?'

Anthuan looked down at the ground and furrowed his brow as if he was thinking seriously. 'I think you're my best mate in the world, Dan,' he replied slowly. 'And I don't want to be hard on you. But I hate seeing people laugh at you like they did today, you know that. So come on, Dan. You're so young still and maybe you should remember that. You could be out having fun tomorrow night, but you don't want to. Do you really think you're ready to race Bolt? I just can't help feeling that if you raced Bolt now, he'd have time to finish the race and eat a cheese sandwich before you came through the line.'

Dan looked at Anthuan with disgust. He felt angry and let down. 'Oh, right, I see. So not even my best mate believes in me. See ya.' And with that, he trotted off down the road and jumped straight on the 215 bus, leaving Anthuan standing alone.

Danny was furious. But, more than that, he was really upset. *Not even Ant believes in me*, he thought to himself. *I'll just have to prove him wrong too.*